PRAISE FOR **MARTians**

✶ "Woolston does a superb job creating a world that is part Kafka and part Orwell … both haunting and unforgettable." *Booklist* (starred review) ✶

"A bleak and eerie, darkly humorous dystopia." *The Bookseller*

✶ "Gorgeous and gut-wrenchingly familiar." *Kirkus Reviews* (starred review) ✶

✶ "A terrifying extrapolation of the here-and-now and, like much of Woolston's fiction, far too close for comfort." *Publishers Weekly* (starred review) ✶

"If you enjoy witty dialogue and sardonic pieces about culture, you are sure to love this book just as much as I did." *Teenreads*

"The sort of book that challenges and possibly changes a reader's worldview." *KirkusReviews.com*

Blythe Woolston's first novel, *The Freak Observer*, won a William C. Morris Debut Award. She is also the author of *Black Helicopters*, which was an American Library Association Best Fiction for Young Adults selection and one of *Kirkus Reviews* Best Books of 2013. Blythe Woolston lives in Billings, Montana, USA.

Find out more about Blythe Woolston at www.blythewoolston.net or follow her on Twitter: @BlytheWoolston

For more great reads, visit www.ink-slingers.co.uk

BLYTHE WOOLSTON
MARTians

WALKER
BOOKS

First published in Great Britain 2016 by Walker Books Ltd
87 Vauxhall Walk, London SE11 5HJ

2 4 6 8 10 9 7 5 3 1

Text © 2015 Blythe Woolston

Excerpts from *The Martian Chronicles* are reprinted by permission
of Don Congdon Associates, Inc. copyright 1950,
renewed © 1977 by Ray Bradbury

The right of Blythe Woolston to be identified as author of this
work has been asserted by her in accordance with the
Copyright, Designs and Patents Act 1988

This book has been typeset in Utopia

Printed and bound in Great Britain by Clays Ltd, St Ives plc

British Library Cataloguing in Publication Data:
a catalogue record for this book is available from the British Library

ISBN 978-1-4063-4139-3

www.walker.co.uk

For that Earthling, Ray Bradbury—
and for butterflies, raccoons, polar bears,
ostriches, and you—with one condition:
always be looking for the ones you need to help

1

Sexual Responsibility is boring.

It isn't Ms. Brody's fault. She's a good teacher. She switches channels at appropriate moments, tases students who need tasing—*zizzz-ZAAPPP!*—and she only once got stuck in the garbage can beside her teaching station. She was a teeny bit weepy that day, but no drunker than normal, and I've wondered more than once what made her sit in the trash bucket, barely big enough around to jam her rump to the bottom, her arms not quite reaching the floor and her legs in an awkward, toes-to-the-ceiling position. It is to our credit that none of us took advantage of her predicament to behave badly. When she waved her arms and shouted, "Get out! Get out!" we did exactly that. And no one picked up her Taser, either to turn it on her in revenge or to wreak amusement on friends and family later.

I'm concerned that today might be a rerun of that episode. Ms. Brody's red, shiny face is more red and shiny than I'd like to see. I believe she might be crying, although she could be using the toilet tissue spooling out of her purse to mop sweat from her brow rather than tears from her eyes. It is hot in here.

This place, Room 2-B, has been my location, Monday through Thursday, during the hours 9 to 16, for the past two years and six months. That's 2,939.5 hours, including at least 419 hours spent on Sexual Responsibility. I fully expected to spend another one year and six months (1,762.5 school hours) in the same place. If you are checking my math, you should know that I've factored in five weeks of school vacation per year and time absent for bathroom visits and food purchasing as allowed. You should also know that I've checked and rechecked my calculations, because I'm bored.

Other students have other hobbies — like violence or using their phones for self-surveillance. I just sit here and do math in my head. I'm good at math, especially ratios and percentages. Those are the foundation of responsible consumer citizenship. Without them, a person can't begin to be a comparison shopper or make adequate use of coupon doubling.

The first morning I was here, Room 2-B was filled to capacity: two students per desk with standing room only along the walls. The room was full of noise and color then, like the pet department at AllMART and for much the same reason:

many live things were all being shelved in the same place. Just as it is appropriate to keep Siamese fighting fish in plastic cups for $7.99, it is appropriate to keep the lot of us here, in Room 2-B, where we learn not only Sexual Responsibility but also Communication, Math, Corporate History, and Consumer Citizenship. Or those of us who remain learn those things. Desks now outnumber students, what with dropping out, moving away, and—though no one talks about it—ending up dead. I've calculated the rate of loss. There will be thirteen of us left on graduation day.

Ms. Brody spools out another yard of tissue. If I knew how many yards of tissue she has stashed, I could predict the future with accuracy. I could tell you if she's going to run out of tissue before she runs out of tears.

The giant screen at the front of the classroom brightens alive, full of the looming face of someone we all know and trust, at least in a telepresence way, our Governor. Sexual Responsibility always starts with the same prerecorded message reminding us of our pledge to be responsible citizens. My lips start moving around the familiar words. But it's out of sync. This isn't the recorded lesson. The Governor's appearing live, in real time on the education network. Words crawl along the bottom of the screen: "portant announcement * Important announcement * Important announcement * Important announc"

I don't see Ms. Brody touch the volume control, but suddenly the Governor's voice is booming from the speakers.

We are all paying attention now, except Ms. Brody, and maybe me, a little bit, because I notice Ms. Brody is focused on the wad of tissue she is crushing in her hand. But really, at this point, the message is so loud we can hear it multiplied and mushified as it rings out in every classroom and spills into the halls. It would require discipline and effort not to hear what the Governor has to say:

Governor: Congratulations, students, yes, congratulations. I'm pleased to announce that you are all, as of this morning, graduated.

My brain does the math: impossible. This message must be intended for another classroom, another school. We here in 2-B have another year and a half before we are fully educated and ready for the future.

Governor: In the interest of efficiency, your school . . . (glances at her phone) . . . Frederick Winslow Taylor High School, is closing permanently as of this date. Each student in attendance will have a personal appointment with the homeroom technician who will provide an e-tificate of graduation and referral to an appropriate entry-level position. We are extremely proud of all of you on this occasion. Welcome to an exciting future. All students should remember that learning is lifelong, and convenient enrollment in online courses can open new opportunities, including exciting careers in high-demand fields like Taser repair specialist and spam dispersal manager.

(Cut to ad.)

Voice-over: Unicorn Online University, a better future for you . . . .

Scene: Smiling person stares at phone. Close-up of screen reveals Unicorn University logo.

Voice-over: . . . . full of new and exciting possibilities.

Scene: Smiling person ascends the steps to gleaming glass building and shows phone with logo to receptionist. Close shot of a freshly minted employee badge followed by scene of elevator moving upward.

Voice-over: All thanks to Unicorn Uni. Go, Uni-Uni!

Ms. Brody grabs the volume control and spins the dial until there is only the faintest fanfare of the music that accompanies the ad.

"Abernathy?" says Ms. Brody, and the first of my 2-B class-mates squeezes between the crowded rows of desks from the back corner to the front. He stands beside Ms. Brody's teaching station while she points to her touch screen. Abernathy checks to see if the content has transferred properly to his phone. When he turns to leave, the door is blocked by a security marshal in black body armor. Abernathy knows the drill. He leans his forehead against the wall and puts his hands behind his back so his wrists can be zipcuffed together. Even though it is awkward for him, Abernathy flips the whole room the bird as he leaves. His heart isn't in it. He's just doing it because it would be impolite not to say good-bye.

As Zoë Zindleman and also numerical ID 009-99-9999, I am accustomed to being the last called forward. I don't mind. I see the advantages. Alphanumeric reality has spared me some flu inoculations and many exceptionally bad lunches. Even better, I have plenty of time to myself. It may look like I'm waiting patiently in line, but I'm actually thinking about whatever crosses my mind.

So I sit and wait to take my turn with Ms. Brody, my turn to graduate, ha! Imagine that.

Exciting.

Wow.

Imagine me, a graduate.

I do try, but it doesn't work. The signal has been disrupted; the screen in my head where I watch my life happen is frozen, pixilated, blank, and blue. Months of days have just been clipped out of my life so the future can happen right now. Knowing what to imagine career- and aptitude-wise is ordinarily covered in the last year of the curriculum, which has been canceled. I don't know what to expect. Anything could happen. It's much worse than that time when there was a live mouse in the refrigerator. That was unexpected—but it didn't really change the whole future, just the tiny slice of the future spent opening refrigerators and knowing that a mouse might jump out but probably won't.

This? This changes all 1,762.5 hours I was going to be in school. It changes all of the hours that were supposed to happen forever.

That is a very uncomfortable thought, so I'm going to stop thinking it.

I focus on the seeping leak in the ceiling at the back of the room. It is a good distraction. For one thing, it's more interesting than the continuous looping advertisement for Unicorn Uni. For another, that drip means something to me. It's been a part of my life for two years. I remember the day the ceiling tiles collapsed in the back of the room. The spongy slabs spurted wet goo all over the room. That disrupted our learning. We got formal texts of apology from the School AdMin, which included time-sensitive bonus discount points to be used on our next purchase from the GnüdleKart Express, which meant "free lunch" that day.

I wonder if we will get any bonus discount points or

special coupons as graduation gifts. I hope so.

"Masterson?" says Ms. Brody, and Bella Masterson, the girl all the girls want to look like, stands up and walks to the desk at the front of the room. She is an amazing walker, Bella, and she knows it so she provides us, her audience, with time to appreciate her skill.

I know Bella's name, but she doesn't know mine. She is always called before I am. It is the natural order of things. And I am more interested in her than she ever could be in me. That is also the natural order of things.

One at a time, the remaining students of 2-B proceed to their individual appointments. Ms. Brody keeps spooling the toilet tissue out of her purse and dropping soggy little wads into the trash bucket. One at a time, the brown drops fall from the ceiling and splash the empty desks at the back of the room. I wonder how many drops have fallen since the leak first oozed along the third-story bathroom pipes and down, through the ceiling of Room 2-B. I can calculate that, although I will need to estimate. My answer will probably be correctish but not accu-price accurate.

I am the very last student in Room 2-B. I step forward to Ms. Brody's teaching station.

"Yokum?" says Ms. Brody, without looking up from her touch screen.

"No, Zindleman," I say. I think Yokum has been gone— six months? Maybe a year? I don't know exactly how long.

I didn't pay that much attention to him when he was here. Why bother with boys? Aside from how they come and go, socializing makes it harder to be sexually responsible. That's what my AnnaMom says, and she knows. I don't remember Yokum's face, but I do remember there used to be a Yokum because the name Yokum comes before Zindleman, or used to, when there was a Yokum.

Ms. Brody taps her screen and then looks up at me while she says, "Zoë, Zoë Zindleman." She scrubs tissue over her eyes, across her cheeks, and under her nose. "Did you know, Zoë, that you are my best student?"

I didn't. I mean, I suspected it. I've seen the result charts for the entire test population and know how my own scores fit into that picture, but no, I never knew for certain that I was the best.

"There was a time, Zoë, when a student like you would be going to university—a real university—after graduation. You could have been an economist or an engineer or an education technician, like me." Ms. Brody's head droops forward, and she covers her face with her hands. "I'm so sorry, Zoë," she says, the words a little muffled by her palms, then she straightens, wipes her face, and continues. "But this is not that time. Zoë, you have been invited to apply for an entry-level position at both AllMART and Q-MART. Please check your phone to make certain that your e-tificate of graduation and your invitations to apply are transmitted."

I do that. They are. I open to confirm receipt. I cloud-archive backups. These are important messages.

Ms. Brody's voice changes again; it's softer, more personal. "Good luck, Zoë. And please accept this gift from me—and your school." She hands me a jumbo-size bag with the AllMART logo on it. Yay! But when I look inside, there is nothing but one old book. They don't sell used books at AllMART. Far as I can see, it is a very weird gift. Maybe Ms. Brody confused it with the trash? It's been a confusing day for all of us.

"Thank you, Ms. Brody. Good-bye," I say.

Ms. Brody tries to smile, but it melts into tears and sweat. She wipes them away and then drops the soggy tissue into the trash bucket.

The school halls are almost empty. There are a few end-of-the-alphabet stragglers like me. There is also a long, snaking line of students wearing plastic riot shackles and zipcuffs. A bus will come soon to take them to the penitentiary. Everyone needs an entry-level position. Everyone needs to start somewhere, get that practical experience, and develop natural skills. Even if, like Abernathy's, the natural skill waiting to be developed is cruelty.

I leave my school and step out into the world. It is strange knowing that whatever tomorrow holds, it is not 2-B.

2

Our house is on the market.

That's why I always come in through the front door. I want to see my home as others see it. I know little stuff can make a big difference to a prospective buyer. I focus on the details. I pinch off a dead daylily. I make certain that the welcome mat is perfectly square with the front door.

Every house on the cul-de-sac—in the whole neighborhood, really—is for sale. But none of those houses are as nice as ours. The landscaping is dead, and the backyard pools are slimy with algae and mosquito larvae. Those people don't even bother to close their doors to keep the raccoons out.

Our lilies are still alive.

It's a little thing, but it matters.

I set the plastic bag with the book in it on the mat and then key the combination into the lock. The slippery bag topples over and the book slides out, pages spread open and ruffled by the hot wind. It looks like a dead butterfly, or it would, if butterflies were more rectangular and had hundreds of papery wings. Sometimes butterflies visit the daylilies by the porch. I have watched them unspool their long sipping-straw tongues and slide them like hollow needles into the secret of the flowers. Then they fly away, or the wind blows them away— it is hard to tell because butterflies seem to have so little control over where they are going. The daylilies are left behind, knocked around by the same wind but rooted in that place. The next day the yellow flower is over, crumpled and damp as a wad of tissue, and the butterfly is gone.

I gather up the book and see the words *"The flowers stirred, opening their hungry yellow mouths."* I look once more at the daylilies shaking in the wind.

They do not look like hungry little mouths to me.

I step into the foyer, where everything is clean and serene.

It took a lot of work and a hired home stager named Jyll to get it to look so inviting. Keeping it that way is not difficult. We just don't let a crumb fall or a drop of water bead on a faucet handle. We live by the eight-hour rule: If something comes in, it must be out within eight hours. This applies to everything from food to the junk mail gleaned from the mailbox. There is an exception for durable goods, like clothes and appliances, although we can't afford those right now. The eight-hour rule prevents clutter. It helps us live as gently as ghosts or manne-quins in our own home.

But today I am bringing things into the house. I have the bag and the book that Ms. Brody gave me. I'm not sure how the eight-hour rule will apply to them. Even though the gift is more than a little disappointing, I'm glad I have it to hold on to. It seems momentous, graduation I mean, and the e-tificate is not . . . monumental. The bag makes it more real. So I carry it with me into the family-great-room and put it down on the polished acrylic table in front of the couch. That table looks like air, only a bit shinier, and the AllMART bag sits there, hovering in space. It becomes the focal point for the whole room, although the wall of dramatic frosted windows framing the purely theoretical fireplace is supposed to have that role. Jyll, the home-staging consultant who whipped us into shape last winter, would not be pleased.

I sit on the uncomfortable couch and fish the remote from where it hides in the cushions. I press the program buttons for my homework channel. I don't think about it. I don't have to. My fingers know what it means when I sit on the couch with the clicker in my hands. But when the screen wakes, it is frozen on a written message:

Unicorn University

SUBSCRIPTION SERVICE

For ordering information, press INFO

I do not press Info. We discontinued all paid television service as part of the new austerity budget. If it isn't free, we don't watch it. Until today that meant I could choose between homework and local round-the-clock news. Now I have one choice:

≡ CHANNEL 42 ≡

Sallie Lee: Hello, viewers, this is Sallie Lee, Channel 42 News, the news you can use, with today's Big Story. Today we have a special guest, our Governor. Governor, today you privatized what was left of the public school system. (Looks directly at the camera.) Congratulations, graduates!

(Governor smiles, says nothing.)

Sallie Lee: Thanks to innovations like that, you have been able to balance the state budget. Congratulations, Governor! That's an accomplishment.

Governor: (Glances at her phone, smiles.) A balanced budget means nothing. I'm not stopping until the budget is zero. Zero is the only balance point that matters. There is no reason to take money away from people who earn it and then provide services they may not want. Why should I steal from your bank account

and make your consumer choices for you? It's nuts.
(Looks directly at the camera and shakes her finger.)
I don't believe in government.

Sallie Lee: Wow!

Yes, wow! I think.

**Sallie Lee: (Looks directly at the camera.) The Governor
is keeping all her campaign promises!**

That's the source of Sallie Lee's moment of wow. Mine is
different. At first my wow! is happy surprise. So *that's* why I
graduated today! It was for the greater good. I'm a tiny piece,
but what happens to me matters! Then my wow! is sad. I feel
for the Governor: how painful it must be for her to reject
government. It is like rejecting herself. Public service requires
heroic sacrifice like that.

I click the remote and turn away from the blank screen.

I've already had so much time to think today, and the stuff
I have to think about is so . . . . shapeless, sleep is most attractive. I stretch out flat on the tile floor of the kitchen. It's the
coolest place in the house. So that's where my AnnaMom finds
me, asleep on the kitchen floor, when she comes home hours
and hours later.

* * *

AnnaMom is holding a big bag with the Yummy Bunny logo on it, and good smells of ginger and garlic are escaping, even though I know the lids on the food are sealed tight.

Yummy Bunny is my favorite. It is also more expensive, so we only get takeaway in the big bag with the red-checkered bunny on it on very special occasions.

"Thanks, AnnaMom! When did they tell you?"

AnnaMom pauses and looks at me. "Tell me? Tell me what?"

"That I'm graduated. Graduated! Really! I've got my e-tificate of graduation and my first job referral. Surprise!" I don't have to tell her to be surprised. I can see that she really, really is. She isn't pretending for the sake of celebration. She would never have dropped the bag full of dinner on the floor unless she was genuinely shocked.

"Zoë, baby, what?" says AnnaMom, and she holds her arms open. We lock each other into a hug that neither of us wants to break, but I notice that there is a trickle of soup leaking out of the bag, which is wasteful—and messy—so I give the little extra squeeze that signals hug:over and then gather the food up onto the counter while AnnaMom blots the wetness from the floor.

She looks up from the tiles, which are shining and so clean a person could eat right off them, if they wanted to, which would be a weird thing to want. "Really, Zoë," says AnnaMom. "Did I hear you right? Did you say you are graduated? With a job referral?"

"That's exactly what I said. Two invitations to apply, actually."

"Wow! Fantastic! This is huge."

I open the lids on the containers and snap the disposable chopsticks apart so we can use them. There is so much food: rice balls and soup and noodles and two boxes of tempura . . . and sticky pickled plums and tiny pink sweets to enjoy with cups of green tea. It's a crazy feast. A big family celebration. And it's also confusing, because my AnnaMom didn't know that I graduated today, so we must also be celebrating something else. The house! The house! We must have sold the house. I wait for my AnnaMom to say it so we can hug again, and probably hop around while we are hugging because Wow! We sold the house.

But that isn't what she says.

"I'm moving," says AnnaMom.

"We're moving?"

"Tomorrow," she says. "I'm moving. I was worried, you know, about how it would be for you here, alone, trying to finish school, but . . ."

". . . now we can go together?"

". . . now it's going to be so much less complicated. For you. Here. I'm not worried."

Me. Here.

"Eat some tempura before it gets soggy," says AnnaMom.

So I do. I pick up a big piece of tempura between the tips of my chopsticks and transport it to my mouth. I'm chewing, but

23

I can't taste anything. I could be eating a wad of toilet paper deep-fried in a lovely light batter.

"This way, you can stay here, rent-free, until the foreclosure. And you can keep the flowers green and everything lovely, just in case, you know, the market improves suddenly. Soup?"

I swallow and take the soupspoon she holds out to me. I can be trusted to live alone but not to feed myself. Ah, AnnaMom. It would be funny if I weren't so scared.

We sit together on the slightly uncomfortable couch. We used to have a very comfy couch, but Jyll, the home stager, said it reeked of routine low expectations and had to be replaced immediately if we wanted the house to sell. All furniture tells a story, according to Jyll. When people see a couch like the one she provided, they imagine fun family togetherness. That's a story that will sell, sell, sell.

Only it hasn't yet. So we need to change the story. I assume that Jyll will show up and haul the couch away, because the story of family togetherness, fun or not, has been canceled. I assume this will happen because I have seen the moving vans come and empty out the other houses on the cul-de-sac. AnnaMom and I just sit and don't say a word about our circumstances.

We do not say, either of us, what we both know is true: She is the reason we are in this situation. She made a choice a long time ago. She chose life, me, Zoë. And now we are both living with the consequences.

24

Anna Meric was a few months older than I am right now when she came to the conclusion she was pregnant. She had tried to come to every other possible conclusion—deadly cancer, anorexia, just losing track of time—but motherhood was headed her direction like a truckload of radioactive bricks, and finally she had to admit it. She admitted it several times, in fact, because confession is good for a person.

About twelve hours after the last time she confessed it, I was born. A couple hours later, Anna Meric, now my AnnaMom, was filling out forms that would shift the responsibility for me to someone else, who wanted it. This was the course of action proposed by the people in charge, and Anna could see the advantages, really she could. But she refused to sign the papers. Her act of defiance surprised her-own-self as much as anyone. Instead of doing what was obviously the best thing for everyone involved, she demanded the forms that would confirm that I was her daughter and she was my mom. While she was at it, she named me. Zoë, that makes sense; it means life. The Zindleman? That she just made up. It was not a name she borrowed from my father. I did have a father, but his approach to the whole matter of me was to admit his part in this fiasco of irresponsibility and then waive all rights.

His name was Ed Gorton.

Gorton isn't a very musical name.

I like Zindleman better.

In some alternative universe, I suppose Ed and Anna

got married and I was the first of many children. In some alternative universe, I was never conceived at all. But in this universe, I'm Zoë Zindleman, whose biological father, Ed Gorton, isn't in the picture.

Anna Meric started over, although her decision to keep me was a complicating factor. It is hard to make a good impression when you walk into a job interview trailing a streamer of toilet paper. It's even harder when the toilet paper isn't stuck to the bottom of a shoe, but is tangled up in the elastic of some barely there underpants along with the hem of a businesslike suit. Anna Meric had the social disadvantage of walking around with her carelessness exposed.

Somehow she managed to overcome that first impression. She got a job. She worked very, very hard. Then Ed Gorton got kicked in the head by an ostrich. It killed him. It's an unusual way to die, but not unheard of. The papers he had signed in the hospital established me as his sole beneficiary. We had money enough to move into this fine house in an excellent neighborhood and live happily ever after. If anyone asked, Anna Meric could honestly explain why the daddy wasn't in the picture with tragic death, which is respectable, although I think she left out the detail about the ostrich.

3

"Hey! You! Last girl! Yes. You. Who else?"

"What?"

"That bus. It isn't coming anymore. The bus you are waiting for."

"How do you know what bus I'm waiting for?"

"We rode that bus together for eight years. I lived across the cul-de-sac."

"Which cul-de-sac?" I say. There are a thousand, two thousand, three thousand cul-de-sacs. Saying that we lived on the same cul-de-sac—it sounds personal, but it might sound personal to a thousand, two thousand, three thousand girls sitting in bus shelters.

"Terra Incognita," he says. "You lived in the beiger house; it is more beige than the other beige house. I lived in the white house."

Our house—*my* house—where I will live alone until I sell it, is painted a color called Aged Pages. It is, I suppose, beiger than the other beige house. I hadn't really thought of it that way, but then, I hadn't really thought of the other houses on the cul-de-sac very much at all. There is a white house too, bone white. So he might be right, but I still have no reason to believe that he knows me or that I should listen to what he has to say about the bus.

"You don't believe me," he says. "That's okay; ask the driver of the next bus. That bus will come in half an hour. That's fifteen minutes after you should expect the bus that used to go to Terra Incognita but doesn't go there anymore. There is no bus to Terra Incognita."

I do not look right or left. It is broad daylight. I'm in a bus shelter outside the doors of AllMART. There are people all around me who will, I hope, intervene if this crazy person who insists he knows about me does anything more disturbing than talk about the color of house paint.

What I really hate is that he seems to be right about the bus. The scheduled time comes and goes. AnnaMom's shoes hurt my feet and her third-best business suit is a sweltering sweatbox. But I look perfect, that's what AnnaMom said: *You look ready for the world, Zoëkins. It's all about the clothes. I'm not worried. Twirl around.* I study the bus map to see which bus

28

I might take that will get me as close as possible to home.

"That map's way out of date."

I don't look around. I do not acknowledge him in any way.

"I can give you a ride. I was going to drive back there today anyway—to pick up some stuff."

The bottoms of my feet hurt. Sweat escapes my bra strap and trickles down, down, down until it soaks into the waistband of the tailored skirt.

"Okay," I say. It may be that I won't last one single day on my own in the world. It may be that I have just accepted a ride from a murderous maniac. But it's a sure thing that I don't want to stand here in this bus shelter, breathing fumes belched out by buses that are never going to where I want to be.

"Did you interview with AllMART?" The maniac is making small talk. It's probably a page in the maniac serial killer handbook: Small talk puts your victim at ease. . . .

"And Q-MART," I say, which is true but is also code for "Lots of people will notice if I go missing"—which isn't as true.

"Wow. You're set, then. You get to choose. Choose AllMART. AllMART is the best. He fishes in his back pocket and pulls out an employee ID badge with the distinctive AllMART logo.

"You say that"—I squint at the name on the badge—"*MORT*, because you work there. If you worked at Q-MART, you'd think that was the way to go."

"Call me Timmer," he says. "I'm Timmer."

"Why does your badge say MORT, then?"

"It's an AllMART thing—there's a system. At work, I'm MORT. To my friends, I'm Timmer. And to prove I am *your* friend, I'll tell you two things. First, do not badger the AllMART badger. It's a bad idea to badger the badger. Second, trust me when I say AllMART is the better choice."

"Despite the name badge thing . . ."

"Despite a *lot* of things. I've been working there for months. I know. I've seen."

"So, you didn't graduate yesterday?"

"Actually, I did. Just like you, but I've been working for a long time. The graveyard shift, mostly—and weekends. I got a family hardship waiver."

"What's a family hardship waiver?"

"Things got hard; they waved. Seriously, you know how it goes."

Yes, I do. When I shut my eyes I can still see my AnnaMom waving her tiny everything-is-normal-and-good wave at me before she looked over the steering wheel and said, *I'm not worried. I'll call when I get work.* Then she drove away and left me standing by the doors to the employees' entrance at AllMART.

He parks in front of the white house on Terra Incognita. The door to that house is wide open.

"Thank you." I'm in a hurry to be gone. I don't look at MORTimmer, but I listen in case his footsteps follow me while I hurry toward my own house. When I get to my door, I glance back. The door to his house is still gaping open, but I can't see him anywhere. I do not stop to pick the dead daylilies. I do not stop to collect the junk mail. I just hurry to press the buttons on the lock and shut the door behind me.

Honestly, the house isn't any emptier today than it was yesterday. The only difference is that today my AnnaMom will not be coming in the door. I am not just alone *now*; I will be alone, maybe, always. I kick off my mom's shoes, but I do not carry them upstairs to place neatly on the shoe rack in her closet. Doing that would only remind me that these shoes are alone too, because the rest of AnnaMom's shoes are gone.

I have spent the day in AnnaMom's shoes, and it sucks.

AllMART is on one side of fourteen lanes of traffic, counting on- and off-ramps. Q-MART is on the other. If the stores were gunfighters, which they aren't, they would be squinting at each other, waiting for the other one to flinch. There is no flinching in mega-merchandising.

When I interviewed, I had to go from one store to the other.

It would have been easy to go from one store to the other with a car, but AnnaMom and the car were far, far away. After my first interview, I set out across the parking lot. First winding through row after row of parked vehicles, then straight across the shimmering desert of empty parking, and up and up and up to a pedestrian bridge suspended like a spiderweb over the interstate. I felt so tiny, like an ant looking for sugar. Did others like me really build all this? The lanes, the lazy-loop curves of the exit ramps, the stores full of everything we want?

When big trucks with trains of three or four loads swept under the pedestrian bridge, they pushed hot wind up and under my skirt. Commuter cars scooted along bright and light as crumpled candy wrappers.

I remembered being in the car with my AnnaMom and feeling the gusts of passing trucks. We came here to do our shopping every week, but I never noticed the bridge. I never looked up and saw any people marching like ants from the AllMART half of the world to the Q-MART half. I never looked up and saw an ant person like me, creeping along meeting other bedraggled, trudging ants. None of us smiling. All of our faces smudged with sweat and diesel soot, all of our steps made on sore feet.

I wondered if the others considered jumping off, falling into the traffic. I had those thoughts, but it wasn't even possible. The pedestrian skyway is built inside a wire-mesh tube. The dirty wind and the hot sun can get in, but nothing bigger than a butterfly can come and go as it pleases.

Before my second interview, I wiped my face, straightened my back, and pretended there were no blisters on my feet. After the interview, after I stepped out the door and into the parking lot, I gave up. I cried, with good reason. I had to cross the bridge again. I had to cross the bridge to get to the bus stop.

So I cried. I cried the whole way from one side to the other. And then, when I got to the bus stop, MORTimmer told me there was no bus to Terra Incognita.

I climb the stairs and go into my bathroom. I peel off the third-best suit and drop it on the floor in front of the shower. I skin off my underwear and toss it into the sink.

During both interviews, I was complimented on my professional dress. It expressed maturity and seriousness. Very positive. However. However, the dress code for an entry-level person with my qualifications is not so rigorous. The uniform is black slacks and white polo that has the AllMART/Q-MART logo smack over my heart. Heels aren't recommended. In fact, they are discouraged—workplace safety, yes?

Oh, yes, health and safety, very important.

They drew blood. First AllMART from my left arm, and then Q-MART from my right arm. I watched the vacutainers fill up with me, dark, red, liquid me. The cells inside will whisper about what I ate for dinner and if I have a secret inclination to be diseased. Corporations have the right to know those things about me, just like they have the right to my school records, aptitude test scores, and psychological profile. The little tubes were whisked away. Then gloved hands (lavender at AllMART, green at Q-MART) pressed a cotton ball on the place where my secrets leaked out and patched me up with elastic tape.

The possibility that I wouldn't be hired for an entry-level job—that was never mentioned. Still, I suppose it might happen. And if it does, I don't know what comes after that.

These are, again, uncomfortable, shapeless thoughts. I step into the shower, and the pinging needles of water drive them away. My shampoo smells of oranges and ginger, just like it did yesterday and the day before that. And my washcloth still has pink and white stripes.

I wrap myself in the old towel that we hide away in case someone will be viewing the house. The towels on the racks, like the little soaps by the sink, never get used. They are props. I've smelled the soaps shaped like roses, and I'm convinced that using them would give a person a rash, so I don't feel deprived. And as for this towel, it has been to the pool and had a lot of other adventures the perfect towels never will. Right now, this adventure towel gets to be what I wear instead of clothes.

I hang the suit in my closet. At least there it won't look as abandoned as it would stranded in AnnaMom's empty walk-in. She used to laugh about how the bedroom she had when she was a kid was smaller than the closet she had now. But now she doesn't have a bedroom or a closet; she is in some place, driving down the highway. If she sleeps in a bed, it will be a strange bed. She is between homes, homeless.

I have been in that place too, but I don't remember it. I was a baby back then, when Anna Meric left that other home where I had grown from a bean into a significant burden.

I think maybe Anna Meric always had more confidence in the future than I have. She's invented a new life for herself, found a new home, a couple of times. But I was always just along for the ride. I never had to decide what happened next. Even now, all I have to do is put some clothes on, go downstairs to the kitchen, and pull last night's Yummy Bunny leftovers out of the fridge, but I'm just standing here wrapped in an old towel, wishing I would hear the rattle of the garage door as it opened. And then AnnaMom would come in and say, *Zoë, baby, I'm home.*

"Whoever was knocking at the door didn't want to stop."

I am reading the book Ms. Brody gave me. It is a story about a brave spaceman who has traveled by rocket ship to Mars. That's who is knocking on the door, the spaceman. The pages are brittle and brownish. It was written so long ago that people thought people might use a rocket to fly to Mars, knock on a door, and expect an answer.

Talk about rude. The guy shows up uninvited, acts all-important, and calls the woman inside a Martian even though that word means nothing to her; it isn't what she calls herself. After the woman slams the door in his face, he starts knocking again. I can hear him knocking. Really, I can. Someone is knocking on *my* front door.

AnnaMom would not need to knock. She knows the combination to the door. The real estate agent would not need to knock either. She knows the combination too. She can get in here whenever she wants — that's why it's important for the house to be show-ready every second. It is hard, though, to imagine anyone who would want to see the house now. Houses show better in the morning light. All the drapes and blinds should be open and strategic lamps should be on . . . that's what sells, sells, sells. But now it is dark and I've closed the blinds and I have only one lamp on to spill a puddle of light on the page I'm reading.

"*Whoever was knocking at the door didn't want to stop.*" I read the sentence again, and the knocking goes on, *PLUNK PLUNK PLUNK . . . PLUNK PLUNK PLUNK . . .* I pull my towel around me tighter and go to stand by the door. I peek at the security vid display. It is too dark out there to see. If I switch the porch light on, whoever is there will know . . . what? I don't know, but it frightens me, the thought of them, whoever they are, knowing.

"Hey, you, it's me!" says a voice on the other side of the door.

That clears things up. That means nothing. That could be said by anyone to anyone. It could be said by a coyote to a cat, by a spaceman to a Martian, by . . .

"Hey, do you got water? I need a shower. The water's gone at my house. I see you got electric, so, if you got water, can I, please?"

"Mort?"

"Yeah, it's me, Timmer."

I turn and push the buttons on the alarm system and

open the locks, one, two, three, then I pull my towel around me tighter once more before I open the door.

"Hello, Mort."

"Hello, Last Girl. Hey, you do got water, I guess, because look at you, in a towel—and your hair still wet."

"I have water. And you can come in for a shower, because, thank you for the ride." And then he steps in the door, and when it shuts, I'm not alone anymore. Although I'm not sure this is better.

"I'll show you the shower," I say, and I lead the way upstairs. Then I go into my room, lock the door, and get dressed. I should have done that sooner. If I had, I could have given him this towel, the old adventure towel, and it would have had the new adventure of wiping water off the skin of a new and different body. That's not going to happen. He's going to grab one of the perfect prop towels to dry off. It will never be the same after that. It will never be so plush and full of promise. It will never be a virgin towel again.

I wonder if the smart thing to do is to stay in my room with the door locked. It seems a little safer, but the door is just a hollow shell of wood around some air, and the lock, well, it's enough to keep someone out if they want to respect your privacy, but it isn't meant for security. It is the sort of security that only exists when you are already secure.

I go downstairs. AnnaMom's shoes are still where I kicked

them off my sore feet. I walk over and pick them up. I should put them away, out of sight. Who is going to see them? Me? MORTimmer when he finishes his shower? The imaginary family looking for the perfect home? I carry the shoes with me into the kitchen, open the trash bin, and drop them into the bottom.

I open the fridge and stare at the takeaway containers. AnnaMom planned ahead when she got so much. Even though she isn't here, she is still feeding me, making certain that I eat — at least until the leftovers run out.

"Thanks." He's standing in the kitchen doorway. His polo shirt is wet, and water is dripping from his hair onto his shoulders.

"I have food," I say. "There's enough if you want some."

"I ate at work," he says.

"So you're not hungry?"

"Didn't say that. Thank you, yes, if you have more than you need."

"It's just leftovers." I pull the containers out of the fridge and notice there is a little bottle of plum wine in there too. I'm not sure why we didn't drink that last night. Maybe if we had shared plum wine it would have felt less like the end of the world.

I divide the food between two plates and warm them, one at a time, in the microwave. Then I carry mine in to sit on the couch. It's not really a thing we do anymore, eating on the couch, but the way we do things doesn't seem to matter much anymore, now that AnnaMom is gone, now that there isn't a we.

Now there is only me, Zoë, and this other person, MORTimmer, sitting on a couch with plates balanced on our knees.

"What's that?" he asks, pointing with his chopsticks at the book hovering on the nearly invisible table.

"It's a graduation present from my homeroom technician."

"Nobody gave me anything," he says.

He leans forward and puts his plate on the table. Then he picks up the book and ruffles the pages slowly. He turns to the beginning of the first story and says, "It's about history, huh? Way back in 1999?"

"I don't think so. I think when they made it, 1999 was far in the future. They thought we were going to go to Mars."

"'When the town people found the rocket at sunset they wondered what it was. Nobody knew, so it was sold to a junkman and hauled off to be broken up for scrap metal,'" reads MORTimmer. "The future—or past or whatever it is—it sounds like now." He sets the book back on the table.

"There is no light at my house, you know; the electric, it's gone."

"How long before that happens?" I ask. "How long before they shut off the power when you don't pay the bill?"

"A month, two, but that doesn't matter. I can show you

how to hook it back up, or I can do it for you."

"Well, why don't you just hook yours back up?"

"Because it's gone. Somebody came and stripped the wires out of the walls. They took some of the plumbing too. You know, to sell. So, no water and no electric. It's pretty much that way in all these houses now."

"They steal wires?"

"Yes."

"And they will steal that way from my house?"

"After a while. I think they wait until nobody is home most of the time."

"Who would buy a house that had been ruined like that?"

"The same people who wanted the houses here before they were ruined: nobody. Nobody is going to live in these houses ever again. When you give up and move on, it's over. Actually, it doesn't matter if you give up or not. It's over. Last Girl, you are the last person in the last living house in Terra Incognita."

"This is good," says MORTimmer. "I get tired of eating nothing but cereal and the food from the AllMART Eateria. It tastes the same every time, you know? So, yeah, there's variety to choose from, but it never changes. When my Grammalita made soup, it was different every time. Sometimes it was okay, sometimes it was the best soup ever, but it was always a surprise. There are no surprises at the Eateria. Every burrito is exactly like every other burrito. That's the AllMART way."

"My mom never made soup. She was too tired after work

for cooking. And there were only the two of us."

"There were seven of us."

"Big family."

"Not anymore. My family is the same size as yours, now. Only one."

I think my family is still two of us, even if AnnaMom isn't here. She is . . . somewhere. She exists.

His plate is clean.

"I'll take that," I say. When I get to the kitchen, I think I'm going to scrape the plates and put them in the dishwasher, but I don't. I just drop them into the garbage on top of the shoes.

"You figure things out fast." MORTimmer has followed me.

"Do you want some plum wine? It's cold."

"Is it good?"

"I think it's good."

"I'll trust you."

One of the kitchen lights is focused on the wineglasses hanging from slender stems. When the imaginary family sees them, they will be enchanted by their party sparkle. I open the little bottle and pour it into two glasses so we each have half.

When I hand his glass to him, he holds it out in an expectant way, so I clink my rim against his. I think we are supposed to say something too, but what?

"I'm glad you trusted me," says MORTimmer. "I'm glad you aren't still sitting in that bus shelter. I was worried about you. It's hard, I know, at first. I'm glad you let me help you."

I'm not sure I trust him. I got in his car. I opened my

front door when I was dressed in nothing but my adventure towel. Those things are true, but those things are not equal to trust.

Soon, the plum wine is gone. I hold out my hand and MORTimmer surrenders his empty glass. Then I throw both glasses, hard, into the sink, where they shatter into an entirely new sort of sparkle party under the lights. I take down two more glasses and throw them too. Very pretty. Very satisfying.

"I need to go now," says MORTimmer. "Graveyard shift."

I follow him to the door, tap on the security pad. 1-2-2-6 A-2-Z, Anna to Zoë.

"I'll come back in the morning," he says. "They might call you tomorrow about the job, but if they don't, don't worry. They might take until Monday." Then he walks away across the cul-de-sac to his car where it is parked in front of the bone-white house where he lived with his big family, even a grandmother who made soup. I never noticed when they were there. Now they are gone. There is nothing to see. I shut the door. I pick up my dead butterfly of a book.

The daylilies that bloomed today are wadding themselves into little damp wads. The ones that want to bloom tomorrow are waiting for the sun.

I climb the stairs, and while I do, I imagine hard as I can that this is just a night when AnnaMom needs to work late. She called. Yes, she called like she always called, to tell me *Just go to bed, Zoë, baby. I'll be there in the morning.* But I can't quite remember it enough to believe it. *You know I love you,*

Zoëkins, whispers imaginary AnnaMom.

"How much do you love me, AnnaMom?"

I love you 37 pink socks and a bowl of cereal. I love you 12 stair steps, 9 long months plus 15 years, 5 months, and 25 days, whispers imaginary AnnaMom. Her math is exactly right. That was how much she loved me.

I stand beside my bedroom window and look out. What I see is dark. There are no lights in the windows of the houses of Terra Incognita. Even the streetlights have gone dark because there is no one on the street to pay to keep them shining.

In the canyon between my house and the house next door, dark shapes are moving through the shadows. Animals. Not pets. There aren't any pets in Terra Incognita anymore. There used to be. But then the time for moving came, and pets were a complication. So the animals got left behind. Maybe it was supposed to be temporary, but it wasn't. The ones that waited died, and the ones that lived went wild. Cats did better than dogs. There were dogs next door, which barked for a while in the garage and then, I guess, died. AnnaMom said it was wrong to leave those animals behind. She tried calling to get animal police to come and collect them, but we didn't have the extra money. I thought maybe we should just open the garage door, but AnnaMom said we couldn't take the chance. Those were guard dogs trained to bite, maybe. And now they were hungry. We couldn't take the chance. We just had to wait. It only took a few days, and then the barking stopped.

Far away, over the horizon, there is a glow of lights from

the parking lots of AllMART. There are still people there. But here? I am the last girl in the last living house. I am Zoë Zindleman. I'm used to being the last one. It gives me time to think, but right now, I don't know what to think, so I pick up the book and start reading again.

On imaginary Mars, butterflies made of fire drink nectar from crystal blossoms. Here in the last living house in Terra Incognita, there are broken wineglasses in the sink.

4

"I said I would come back," he says when I open the door.

That's true. He did, but I never said I wanted that.

"Graveyard shift ends at seven, and then I stopped by the Warren and made sure everything was cool for you moving in. I thought you'd be up by now."

"I don't know what you are talking about."

"When you start work, you can't live here anymore. You need to move, so you should live with me, us, in the Warren."

"This is my house."

"It is for another few weeks."

"You still live here." I point to the white house across the cul-de-sac.

"I don't live here. I come back here sometimes. And now that the water is gone, it's not worth the trip. If I start double-shifting, it won't even be possible. I mean, the commute—when would I sleep?"

"What if I don't get a job? What then?"

"You have *two* work referrals. You have twice as much chance of being hired as most people. The only people with a clearer sense of future employment than you are wearing prison tattoos. If Tuesday rolls around and you haven't got a job—that isn't going to happen. What is going to happen is I'm going to use your water and then sleep, and you are going to start packing up what you need, because the phone is going to ring, and then you will be moving to the Warren, which is conveniently located so close to both AllMART and Q-MART that we never hafta turn the lights on—the parking lot secur-ity lights keep it bright as day all night long. I'm going to shower. I brought you a jam doughnut." He hands me a bag and starts up the stairs like they are his stairs and this is his house. He does that while I stand there holding a bag full of squished jam doughnuts, red smears and flattened buns.

After our last dinner together, AnnaMom packed her things while I watched.

"I wish we had some of the family stuff," said AnnaMom. That stuff is all packed away. While she was staging our house, Jyll took all that stuff—my baby pictures, our refrigerator magnets, the collection of hard-to-find ostrich-related art—and locked it away in her unit at SecurIt Safe-Keeping Storage. Jyll said she understood the sentimental value of those things, but they couldn't be in the house. People want to imagine their own happy future, and it's too much trouble for them to go through the thought process of replacing my toothless smile with whatever they think is cute. Jyll never did understand, exactly, the ostrich thing, even though we tried to explain. She thought it was some sort of morbid memorial or we were members of an ostrich cult.

"Look," said Jyll, "I don't let people keep crucifixes on the wall or carvings of Kali on the mantel. No ostriches. I don't care if they are good luck. You don't need luck to sell this house; you need me."

Jyll might have been wrong about that.

Right or wrong, all the family stuff is locked away in storage, which made AnnaMom's packing more efficient. All she packed were her work clothes and personal items. While she zipped toiletries into little cases and tucked shoes snugly into a suitcase, she said, "You can use our stuff when you set up your first apartment. And the money from when the house sells, that all goes to you after the sales commission. It will be your nest egg."

In her head, I think AnnaMom was imagining a nest egg laid by an ostrich. The nest egg I really have is something about the size of a human egg, which, as I learned in Sexual

47

Responsibility class, is so small you can fit 200,000 of them into an olive.

"You should be packing," he says when he comes back downstairs. I am still standing by the door with the bag of doughnuts. How long have I been standing here? How long does it take a boy to shower? He rubs his wet hair with a virgin towel and says, "I can help you if you have a lot."

A lot? Do I have a lot? I don't know if I have a lot.

"Do you got boxes?"

"In the garage. For when we move . . ."

"This is then. This is when you move. But we should eat first," and he takes the paper bag gently out of my custody. "Do you have coffee? I woulda brought some, but it woulda got cold, you know? Coffee?"

"Coffee?"

"Coffee," he says again, like he's talking to a goldfish. Then he walks into the kitchen. I swim along after, through the arches of my goldfish castle, from one part of my bowl to another.

We do have coffee, in wonderful tiny capsules that keep it fresh until the coffee machine jaws bite down and inject boiling water through hollow metal fangs and the coffee drips dripsdrips drips down, smelling like hazelnut and butterscotch and whatever it is that coffee, plain coffee, smells like.

In the almost-a-minute it takes to make coffee, I say, "The packing. What do I need?"

"We got you mostly covered at the Warren, but some clothes for when you aren't at work, personal stuff, bring that. Personal stuff. And you should bring your own bowl and spoon. That way there won't be arguments about dirty dishes so much."

I open the cupboard where the bowls live, stacked into beautiful little pagodas. In front of them there is a little row of chopstick holders: little bunnies, little kitties, little fish, all curling just so, just right, just perfect. We never used them to hold our chopsticks. We just had them because they are *kawaii*—so cute. I shut the cupboard and open the drawer where we keep the plastic dishes. There, at the back, is a plastic bowl with a row of pink bunnies running along the rim. At the bottom of the bowl is a full moon, smiling up at me, smiling up at the bunnies. I've seen those bunnies, that moon, so many times. How much do you love me, AnnaMom? *I love you a pink bunny bowl, and a pink kitty comb, and a little silver spoon just the right size for your little baby mouth.*

I open the silverware drawer and look through all the sections, but the little silver spoon isn't there. Maybe AnnaMom packed it away in a gray plastic bin and Jyll took it away to Safe-Keeping Storage. Is that what happened to my spoon, AnnaMom? *It doesn't matter if a mean girl broke your kitty comb, Zoëkins. She didn't break your heart. I know. I know she didn't break your heart. I know because I keep it in my own heart.*

How much do you love me, AnnaMom? *I love you all the*

doorknobs and a bubble bath. I love you a pink-striped wash-cloth. I love you all that.

I choose one of the other, ordinary spoons.

MORTimmer puts a mug of coffee into my hand and then he balances a squished doughnut on the rim. Some of the red goo clings to his thumb until he wipes it on the towel draped around his shoulders. That's another virgin towel so very ruined.

I pack while MORTimmer sleeps on my mother's bed. Instead of a box, I use the bag Ms. Brody gave me. I put the book at the bottom, then my pink bunny bowl and my ordin-ary spoon, six pairs of clean underpants, my pajamas, my toothbrush, my striped washcloth, and the adventure towel. I look in my closet where my school clothes smile like flowers dipped in sugar. I shut my eyes and brush my hand along those clothes like I did each morning before I went to school, when I needed a costume that would shelter me, hold me, make me happy. They exhale a little fresh scent, just like they are sup-posed to do. Still, no sleeves cling to my fingertips. Nothing says, *Pick me! Pick me!* so I can open my eyes and smile and think, *Yes! This! Kawaii!* So I open my eyes and I choose a sweater, because it might get cold later. AnnaMom always said that, every day: *It might get cold later, ZeeZeeBee. Take a sweater.* So I choose a sweater, and then I shut the door and leave the rest of the clothes wilting in the dark.

* * *

50

My phone sings. I answer. It is a robocall that says, "*Hssshhsh* . . . Zindleman, Zoh-EE, *sskksh* . . . you are part of the AllMART family!" Then the phone sings again and I think it might be AllMART calling, but it is the text message confirmation of my job offer, which requires a response acknowledgment.

I walk into the master bedroom, where MORTimmer is stretched out diagonally across the bed with a pillow clutched in each arm. There is still a little water pooled in the hollow of his lower spine, which surprises me, but there it is, a pearl of water come to rest.

My phone sings again, but I thumb it quiet fast, just sneaking a look at the caller ID. It isn't my AnnaMom. I step into my own room, shut my door, and check the message. "It's always Q-MART! Q-MART is your savings store, all you want and even more. . . . This message is for . . . *click* ZOO ZINDLEMAN *click*. Congratulations! . . . *click* . . . ZOO . . . *click*. . . . You have been selected for a position with Q-MART." Then it's the job offer text awaiting my reply.

I have a choice to make, a great big might-matter-for-the-rest-of-my-life choice. On one hand, I don't want MORTimmer to think I listened to him and chose AllMART because I respect his opinion. On the other hand, I do not want to accept any job offered to a person named ZOO.

"Last Girl? I heard the phone." He is standing on the other side of my hollow bedroom door.

I stand up and say, "Yes. It was about the jobs. I will start on Monday at AllMART." I reply yes to the text.

"I can help you pack now," he says.

"I think I'm done," I say, and I open the door. "I think I have everything." I hold out the AllMART bag. I don't mean for him to take it, but he does; then he turns and walks down the hallway toward the stairs. He's wearing a shirt now, but I still wonder about that drop of water and gravity and other unnameable things.

"No boxes?" he calls up the stairs. "A suitcase?"

AnnaMom took the suitcases. She knew what she needed, what she wanted, and she took it.

I'm still here.

I don't know what I need. But I know what I want, and it isn't here.

"The bag. It's all in the bag."

"Well, if you have food, we can bring that. Food is useful. Especially cereal."

The Warren isn't a house. It's a dinky, dusty, abandoned strip mall. MORTimmer parks his car in a delivery alley between some Dumpsters. Here, in the back, all the doors are gray metal rectangles in the windowless wall. The business names are written in black block letters on the doors. It isn't inviting, but then it isn't meant to be. The alley is not the face that the stores show to the customer.

"Shut your eyes," says MORTimmer. "I want it to be a surprise." He pulls open a door. I don't know why I should have to close my eyes; it is so dark in there I can't see a single thing. Then he takes my hand and says, "Come on." I don't shut my eyes. I don't pull my hand away from his either. He pulls me into a small, hot space full of rumbling noise. The heavy door behind us clicks shut.

"You can open your eyes now," he says. It is so dark he has no idea if my eyes are open or shut, but he's pulling me forward, three steps and a little stumble, and then there is the light of a door opening in front of us.

My eyes adjust.

We are in one of the stores. No, not a store, a public laundry. I've never been in a place like this. The thought of it makes me cringe a little. Imagine, washing my underpants where some stranger had just washed—who knows what? Sheets full of body dirt? Baby pants smeared with all the smelly things that come out of babies? I smell hot clothes, detergent, and drains. The faint smell of dirty water reminds me of Room 2-B. It does not remind me of home. It's another thing I've lost, the quiet growl of the dryer on a cold night while AnnaMom and I eat microwave popcorn in the kitchen and the whole world smells of fabric softener and butter.

Rub-a-Dub-Tub. Someone has painted a mural over the windows. Blue birds are hanging striped towels, pink and green and white, on a clothesline. Painting on the windows is very low budget / low return as far as advertising goes. I'm not impressed. I am not persuaded.

"This is 5er."

A little boy is perched on top of a service counter beside a cash register. He isn't wearing anything but underpants. He has long, bony feet and long, bony toes. I look away. Behind him, a screen is flickering pictures. The sound is turned off, but I can read the crawl along the bottom. I can't help myself. I can't ignore a screen. . . .

. . . closed due to smoke from fires in the area. Traffic is being diverted. Don't depend on GPS updates. Depend on Channel 42. All the answers are on Channel 42.

"5er. Hey, man. This is Zoë. This is the last girl I told you about. She lives with us now. Say hi, okay? Say hi."

The little boy puts one hand out. He doesn't look at me. He doesn't say anything.

I put my hand out. Maybe I'm supposed to shake hands. . . . The kid jerks his hand away and hides it behind his back. He shuts his eyes tight.

"It takes 5er a while to get used to new people. Doesn't it, man? But don't worry. It's okay. It's all okay. We shower back there." MORTimmer points at a garden hose hanging from the ceiling. There's no curtain. Just a garden hose and sprinkler nozzle hanging over a drain in the floor. "We got a toilet. And sinks. We talked about maybe stealing a bathtub or inflatable raft and setting up a cool pool-and-shower deal, but it isn't practical, you know?"

"You live here?"

"This is the Warren. It's a good place to live. Safe. Close to AllMART. Come on. Let me show you." He walks behind the counter and opens a door to another room, small. There is a metal desk with an office chair on top of it shoved into the corner. The rest of the floor space is covered with a mattress and a snarl of blankets. "This is our bedroom," says MORTimmer. "You can put your stuff in one of the desk drawers."

"I'm supposed to sleep here? On the floor with you?"

"Well, at least until I can get you another bed, you can sleep with me and 5er, yeah."

"No. Look, I'm sorry, but no. Can you just take me home? This is a mistake. I want to go home."

"Home? Terra Incognita?" He puckers his mouth and sighs. "No can do at the moment. I gotta go ta work. You just sit tight, here, with 5er. We can talk when I get back."

"I need to charge my phone."

MORTimmer points to a charging pad sitting on the counter beside a pyramid of tiny soap packets.

"Thank you." I place my phone on the charger and see the blink of light that means it is sipping energy.

"She isn't going to call," says MORTimmer.

Then he leaves like that's all there is to it. Like he knows me, my AnnaMom, or the future.

5

When the door closes behind MORTimmer, I know I can just walk out the door myself. I can leave. Nothing is stopping me. Except—I don't know what I would do once I passed through that door and it closed behind me. I want to be home, but I don't know how I'd get there. So I sit down on a stiff plastic chair and stare at the screen. There are many things happening in the world; I see them, one after the other, and the words crawl by. I imagine very hard that I am at school. That whiff of bad water, the screen, the crawl of words along the bottom. It is easy to imagine that I am really, truly in Room 2-B and everything is not changed.

For the first time in days, my knotted thoughts untie. For

the first time in days, I feel comfort. I let the screen tell me about the world. I open my eyes and that's all I have to do.

≡ *CHANNEL 42* ≡

Breaking news! Special report!
With Chad Manley and Sallie Lee!

Chad Manley: **Tonight might be a good night for stargazing.**

Sallie Lee: **Wish upon a falling star!**

Chad Manley: **But it will be satellites, *not* stars, falling. It's called satellite rain. And the forecast is for showers. Here to explain is satellite rain expert stratusmeterologist Gavin Kelly.**

Scene: **Gavin Kelly walks briskly down a hall, because that's what experts do, they walk briskly, in halls. Then, depending on what they are expert in, they may sit at a desk, or a gloved hand may fill minitubes with measured doses. Gavin Kelly, stratusmeterologist, fills no minitubes. We see his hands over a keyboard, he waves at the display screen, and we see what he sees, an endless scroll of numbers.**

The numbers fly past so quickly I can't begin to read them, which makes me nervous. But I don't need to process those numbers; they have been understood by the expert who explains it all using animation.

> *Scene:* **Deep space around the earth, satellites migrate on blue solar-cell wings. They are invisible to us, but we have no secrets from them. Their eyes are complex. Our whispers make their golden foil tremble, and they connect our echoes each to each. Without them, we couldn't order a pizza.**
>
> **But sometimes, sometimes the winds of gravity or the tides of sunlight push the little crafts off course. It is the smallest error made a billion times, growing bigger and bigger and bigger. A shave of an electronic cent stolen a billion times is a million dollars.**

I recognize the phenomenon: It's called feedback runaway. Sometimes people call it a chain reaction, but a chain reaction just plods along. Feedback runaway is explosive, especially in human beings. When people fall into feedback runaway loops, there are boom-and-bust cycles in the markets. People rush to the stores to buy three lifetime supplies of vacu-packed dehydrated celery. But this is not about people and money; this is about satellites.

A golden wing is in the path of another satellite. Smash! The mechanical butterflies collide, shatter, and fall, a sparkle party in the dark.

Scene: **Channel 42 News studio**

Chad Manley: **Ha-ha! It's no laughing matter. This means further telecommunication disruptions.**

Sallie Lee: **Local fiber-optic cable will not be affected, but cross-system data flow may be interrupt—**

The screen goes blank and fills with static.

Chad Manley: **Ha-ha, haha. That was our production technician Sanjay. Gotcha!**

Sallie Lee: **Got *us*!**

Chad Manley: **What a tease!**

Sallie Lee: **Of course you can count on Channel 42 for uninterrup—**

(Static fills the screen again.)

Sallie Lee: Our apologies. That was not funny, Sanjay!

(CUT TO COMMERCIAL)

Scene: Black screen

Voice one (male voice): Don't lose touch. Opt for fiber optics.

Voice two (female voice): Fiber optics? Isn't that old-fashioned?

Voice one: Yes . . . if dependability is old-fashioned. Satellite transmissions are fine for moving data, but what about something far more important? What about love? Choose fiber optics for messages that matter. Perfect security. Perfect transmissions. Perfect. Love.

(Tiny print scrolls past in a blur: "Speed of transmission and data security cannot be guaranteed. Seven-year contract. Activation and roaming fees additional.")

Scene: Channel 42 News studio

Chad Manley: And now, breaking news: A tragic custody case is unfolding.

Sallie Lee: Yes, custody battles are always heart-breaking, but this one has a twist—there is a 507-pound tuna at the center of it.

Chad Manley: Sallie, I know there are plenty of custody battles fought over the family pet.

Sallie Lee: This tuna isn't a family pet.

Scene: Interior of industrial freezer. Giant frozen fish are stretched out on a stainless-steel table.

A man wearing a hairnet, sanitary gloves, and white coat stands by one of the fish. There is a tight shot of the tag in the tail fin: a scan code, a number, and unreadable letters.

Man in lab coat: (Incomprehensible words)

Crawl, English translation: "This is not a grave. This is a valuable fish." COULD BE WORTH one and a half million dollars!

Scene: Cut to laughing girl blowing out candles on a birthday cake. The GIF loops. It's like the candles can never be blown out.

Sallie Lee: Right after her sixteenth birthday, Delores Perdita Cash boarded a transpacific flight for her first spring break. Her family never saw her again. She was in seat H8 of fateful Flight 815.

Chad Manley: You remember Flight 815, don't you, Sallie? We kept all our Channel 42 News viewers up to the minute on the search for the wreckage.

Sallie Lee: Yes, Chad, up to the minute for all seven months of the search, and . . .

Scene: Flickering candles on a beach. . . . the one- and two-year anniversaries of the tragedy.

Chad Manley: There's been a new development.

Sallie Lee: The tuna-custody case?

Chad Manley: When the tuna was caught deep in the Pacific Ocean, it had a plastic Baggie inside it. The contents of the bag included a prescription bottle; the name on the label? Delores Perdita Cash.

Sallie Lee: After all those years, her family finally has closure.

Chad Manley: A *chance* for closure. (Dramatic pause) The fishermen refuse to release the tuna to the family for burial.

Sallie Lee: Wow, I know I'm supposed to be objective, but that is *inhuman.* How can they be so cruel?

Chad Manley: The tuna might bring 9.7 million yen on the auction market.

The man in the freezer: This is a valuable fish.

Chad Manley: We'll be following this story.

Sallie Lee: You bet we will, Chad. Because Channel 42 viewers want to know.

At the hour, the cycle begins again: the same stories in the same order—only the ads have changed. This hour they are all for Bats of Happiness, the genuine guano fertilizer. Perfectly organic, perfect in every way: Bats of Happiness.

I remember the day AnnaMom and I planted the day-lilies in front of our house. She spooned dark dirt out of the bag with the red bats printed on it. *This will feed our flower babies, ZeeZeeBee. Do you want a bite? NO! I don't want the flowers inside you to grow out of your ears. And also it's bat poop. Bat poop is good food for flowers, not my Zoë. You should eat sugar violets and vegetable puffs.*

After that, I look at the screen, but I don't see anything.

6

Timmer carries food when he returns from work—a paper Eateria bag full of burritos. He hands one to me. It feels heavy, damp, and pretty sad. Timmer folds a foily paper wrapper back, takes a bite, and swallows without chewing. Then he tears open a little packet of hot sauce and squirts it on the food. 5er unrolls his burrito bundle and picks through the rice, looking for beans. He has the posture and table manners of a wild ape. I'm not hungry. It seems like I ought to be, but I'm not. I just stand there, holding the burrito, which isn't hot or cold and doesn't demand immediate attention.

"How did you find this place?"

"I didn't find this place. Raoul found it. Then Raoul found me. I was still waiting for them to come back. I still thought

65

that was the deal. So I was living there in Terra Incognita right across from your beiger-beige house." He looks at me like I'm supposed to say something. But what? That I never noticed that he was there, not ever? Not when he had a family, not when he didn't. That if you asked me last year who else lived on Terra Incognita, I might have said, *The people next door have scary dogs*, but I didn't know their names.

"For a while I just took care of things, you know? I still had school. I'd already got the family hardship waiver job at AllMART, so work felt like normal. But then, there were hours and hours of being alone. The first days, it was okay. My Grammalita, she never threw any food away, so there were all of these little lumps of leftovers in the freezer. I'd microwave those and the house would smell like dinner, sort of. But it was so quiet. I could leave my shoes in the hallway and nobody yelled about how that could kill Grammalita if she tripped on them and broke her hip, and how she would suffer and die, and how that would always be on my conscience. So there was no yelling, but there was nobody to talk to either. Man, I hated being home. I hated it so much, sometimes I just slept in my car in the parking lot. But then I'd go rushing back to the house the next day because—what if they came back? What if they came back and I wasn't there?"

Those words echo inside of me. Yes, what if AnnaMom comes back? She might come back. What if she comes back and I'm not home?

Zoë-woey, I'm not worried. Don't you worry.

But what if?

Zoë! Shush! Don't think about that. Don't you say one more word about that!

"It still sucked, sitting there in that house with nobody else. And when the bus stopped running, then I needed more money for gas. I was just lucky I had the car. You know? Without the car, I woulda been screwed."

Don't think about that, says imaginary AnnaMom. But Timmer's words are making shapeless, uncomfortable ideas hatch in my heart like spiders. *I didn't know about the bus,* says imaginary AnnaMom. *The bus didn't matter anyway. You are safe. You are sitting on an orange plastic chair. You have a burrito. You are not waiting in a bus shelter for a bus that will never come. You aren't like those dogs that stopped barking. Don't think about those dogs. Don't think about when they stopped barking.*

"So I saw how the guys were coming to the houses to steal the electric and the pipes, and I thought maybe I could get some gas money that way. So I drove around neighborhoods looking for a place where the houses were empty but fresh. Wandering like that was burning gas, but I ignored that fact. I didn't know what I was doing, but I did it anyway. I just broke a window and climbed into a house, and then I kicked through the wallboard by an outlet. I woulda probably fried myself, but somebody had already thrown all the breakers, so the wires weren't hot. Anyway, I just grabbed the wires and started ripping them out, right through the wallboards. It wasn't easy, but it was satisfying. I got into it, and I was yelling and swearing and kicking holes in the walls just because I could. Then I turned around and Raoul was standing there with a pipe wrench in his hand, and one of his choices was to use that wrench to bash in my head. But that isn't the choice he made. He just slapped me down with his bare hand, and then he dragged me out to his truck and explained some shit to me—like how that was his mark spray-painted on the door over the address, and how if it had been anybody else I would be dead right there, because that's what happens when the rules get broke.

"Then he brought me here, to the Warren, and he told me how it was going to be. He told me how it happened one day when he was off-loading the copper wire he'd stripped out of a sad cul-de-sac the night before. He looked over the scrap yard fence and saw this place, the Warren, a ghost mall full of ghost stores. He figured it had been stripped years ago. I mean, it's right next to the scrap yard, right? Talk about convenient. But Raoul, he thought, What the heck? Who knows? And so he drove over here and had a look around. It was weird. The windows weren't broken. The doors weren't forced open. Far as he could tell, there was all kinds of stuff just waiting to be collected and sold. It seemed impossible that somebody wouldn't have already marked it and stripped it, but it was just as impossible that it hadn't been bulldozed down years before, to make room for more AllMART parking or an expansion of the scrap yard or a vacant lot full of weeds. Raoul made his marks on the parking lot, on the walls and the sidewalks, and on the windows and doors that were still there, still shut. But when he got home that night, Raoul did some due diligence. He did some research. He got online, did a little poking around, and found out that the place was all hung up in legal proceedings. It was a pretty low-priority case, though, and nothing had budged for a long, long time. The next morning, Raoul bought the whole place for back taxes, which was less than the cost for gas to drive out to the neighborhoods.

"He went there the next day with his crowbar in hand and popped the lock open on one of the delivery doors. Then he walked into the place like he owned it, which he did. He just walked around. He saw the empty places and the naked mannequins. He looked into the ice cream store that some-body was remodeling so it could be church. The sign on the ticket window said 'Join us for our first service!!!' but the date on that sign was five years ago. He saw the bright painted pillars and the tile benches. And it seemed like a good place. He didn't rip anything out. Instead he put his mark on the doors and left everything just like it was.

"A week or so later he found me and didn't kill me. Raoul built a fire in the chiminea and we sat beside it on the patio of the abandoned ice cream parlor. We talked all night while smoke floated up to the sky. We decided I should live here, in the Warren. It's close to AllMART, so that saves time and money. And it is safe, since it belongs to Raoul. Nobody is going to mess with Raoul. Raoul would stop by and we'd hang out, and that was cool. When I said it was kind of weird and lonely sometimes, Raoul said, 'Well, you can change that. You find some others who need to live here, and you bring them in. Be generous and on the lookout for the weak and the powerless.' That's why I saw you that day at the bus shelter; I was looking. I was looking just like Raoul told me to look."

7

It has been a long time since I've felt so nervous. Maybe the first day of high school? My first day in 2-B? That could be it, the mix of I-know-I'm-supposed-to-be-here and I-don't-know-how-I-belong-or-what-it-means-to-be. I'm at the employee entrance conscientiously early, comfortably early. So I just stand and wait and watch the sky change color, from cement to pink and then back to cement. I'm part of a thin little layer between the cement sky and the cement under my feet. A squished paper cup, a candy wrapper, and me.

While I wait, other new trainees arrive: some quiet, some nervous, others probably like me—nervously quiet. Some faces I recognize from passing by in the halls at school. I don't know

71

the people behind the faces. The only other person from 2-B is Bella Masterson, and if she remembers me, she doesn't show it. I wonder where all the rest of them have gone. Each to where their talents are needed. I remember Abernathy in the zip-cuffs waiting for the bus to the penitentiary. That was right for Abernathy, as far as I can tell. So AllMART must be right for me.

The doors open and we file in and follow the signs and wait in line. We are all very good at waiting in line. We have manners. There is an AllMART badge for each of us. It will be our ID, our key, our face to the world.

ZERO.

My badge says *Zero*. I start to point out the mistake, and then I remember what Timmer told me about being MORT: Don't badger the badger. He never said why, exactly, but I think this isn't the time or place to complain. I'm sure there will be an opportunity to get it fixed later, without holding up the line.

I shuffle to the next station, the employee register. I look at the diagrams and present my name tag to the scanner. Green text flashes on the screen: Z. Zindleman has entered the building. Then the screen goes dark to protect my privacy. A green light flashes above an interior door, guiding me to my destination.

Today's destination is a large room full of desks, like Room 2-B, except cleaner, newer. The vid screen at the front, so familiar, is playing silent flash ads with occasional reminders: "Your smile is the AllMART welcome mat. Put the smile in AllMART." It doesn't make much sense, but then metaphors hardly ever do. Ads and reminders don't have to make sense in the ordinary way. It's just a little friendly flash of insight to get our brain cells synced. I learned that in Consumer Psychology.

I bet everyone else in this room knows that too, because they are all here. We are alike in more ways than our employee badges. We are all smiling. We are all lucky to have this opportunity. Our smiles are AllMART's welcome mats.

The door opens. The room, which was already silent, gets quieter.

"Hi, I'm Dawna Day, your personal human-resources manager, and I'm so very happy to welcome all of you. I know you are nervous, but you shouldn't be. Just stop that right this minute!" She laughs, and, like magic, I'm not nervous anymore. "Each day here at AllMART starts with us standing up proud. Research has shown that people who put their arms in the air have better self-esteem. So we do that, because we should be proud to be part of AllMART." She touches a remote and the vid screen view pops to life. Happy faces, a happy crowd, all gathered in a green meadow somewhere, the blue ocean shining in the distance. The crowd sings the AllMART jingle and does a simple dance routine while the words that match the gestures crawl along the bottom of the screen:

Each does a little part, But all of us are AllMART.
clapclapclap clapclapclap, **AllMART!** *clapclapclap*
clapclapclap, **Let's start!**

It's on a loop, and at the end of the second time through, Dawna Day says, "Stand up! Stand up! Join in! Join in!" When we all finish *clapclapclapp*ing, Dawna Day, my personal human-resources manager, is smiling, and seeing her smile makes me smile. She pauses the vid screen. "Don't you feel great? I know you do. Every one of us feels great! Before we get started, does anyone have concerns?"

I recognize that sort of question as a formality, but Bella in the front row does not. She raises her hand. Dawna Day is looking at a teaching device. If she wanted to be asked questions, she would be looking at us to communicate receptivity and invite interaction. She isn't. Bella begins waving her hand to make herself more noticeable.

"Excuse me, there's an error on my name badge. My name is Bella. . . ."

"There is no error." Dawna Day's voice is crisp. She still does not look up from her teaching device.

"It should be Bella, but it says Belly. . . ."

"The names on the badges are a convenience for the *consumers*, should they need to communicate a failure of service. You can be certain that your badge is correctly linked to your permanent records." Dawna Day is looking at Bella who still thinks there has been a mistake.

"But my name is Bella. I'm Bella Masterson."

Dawna Day exhales a long cleansing breath and glares. "Certainly you can understand this. The badges are unique identifiers. You, *Belly*, can't be *Bella*, because another member of the AllMART family is already *Bella*."

"Can I change it to something else? Something more . . . me? Could I be . . . ?

"No. Your name badge will not be changed. Do you understand the cost of unnecessary changes? You are an AllMART employee. Wear your badge proudly. Now, unless we move on, I must make a charge against your future earnings to pay for the time you have wasted." Dawna Day is smiling—at least she is showing her teeth—while the final word hisses in the otherwise silent room.

Belly shrinks into her desk like a snail into a shell.

Timmer's advice was good: Don't badger the badgers. Just be ZERO instead of Zoë. Just be MORT instead of Timmer. Just be quiet. And smile. I hope that other Zoë out there is enjoying my name.

Dawna Day taps her teaching device, and an authoritative voice rumbles from hidden speakers: "There is no such thing as graduation, not really. In today's rapidly spinning world, we must all be lifelong learners. AllMART supports lifelong learning. That is why we encourage you to take advantage of the special discounts offered to AllMART employees through Unicorn University."

The voice changes to a quick talker, the kind who delivers disclaimers and side-effect warnings in advertisements.

"Unicorn University is proud to provide you with today's programmed education."

Today's instruction starts with a short cartoon featuring the familiar face of Buzzy Bee, the buzz-in–buzz-out bee in the SpeedyMed ads and the romantic lead on *Days of Our Hives*. He is greeted with a murmur of sighs. He is *kawaii*, I guess. I'm not an Otakusexual—although I respect toonophilia as a sexually responsible choice. Heroic Buzzy wears a tiny leather jacket and zips in at the last minute to make things right. His appearance in the training vid is a little different, though. He isn't making the girl bees swoon with his amazing stinger swagger.

Buzzy has big eyes, which should be anime-adorable, but the closer we get to his eyes, the more it looks he has a beehive inside them, hexagonal cells, each with another Buzzy Bee inside, and inside that Buzzy Bee's eyes, another hive. I am relieved when the repetition stops midzoom after implying a universe of Buzzys without actually, you know, spending the rest of my life going deeper and deeper.

The screen switches back to the smiling, cheering employees: *clapclapclap.* Dawna Day gestures, so we stand up and join in. It does feel good to put my hands in the air. I do feel good about myself. I'm great. Of course I feel that way. That is the whole point of practicing self-validating postures: Smile and you will be happy; put your hands in the air and grab some self-esteem.

Buzzy Bee returns and beckons us through the doors

of AllMART headquarters. It is a beautiful building, made of nothing but crystal-clear glass. The people who work there are beautiful. They wave at Buzzy Bee, even though he isn't really there. Buzzy flies high into the soaring glass chambers of the floors above. Finally we are way up in the sky, peeking down at the whole AllMART corporate campus spread out below, perfect and glittering. Glowing clouds spell out the names of the enterprises that are all little parts, just like me.

Unicorn Uni is a division of AllMART. So is SpeedyMed. Even Bats of Happiness, which provides essential nutrients that help grow the lettuce sold in AllMART's FarmFresh Produce department. Everything is connected to everything else, and that means everything depends on me.

The music for the cheer rises. I stand and join in. . . .

I may be just a little part,
But I pledge my beating heart
To AllMART.

Buzzy Bee the animated hero takes us on a tour of the store, which is laid out like all AllMARTs everywhere. We zoom up and down the aisles, and I can feel how the pieces fit together. It makes sense to me. If Buzzy Bee came through the ceiling, plucked me up, and dropped me in another AllMART where it was night instead of day, I would be right at home. It would be perfectly familiar. I will never be lost. What a comfort.

✔ BETTER KNOW A PRODUCT: Casual-Wear Polo

Close-up: An AllMART uniform polo shirt

Voice-over: You know that uniform you wear? It's proof that AllMART cares.

Scene: Zoom into the fabric of the shirt. Slow dissolve to image of deep blue ocean seen from the perspective of a satellite. Switch to the surface of the water and view of factory ship, shining white and blue, with the AllMART logo branded on the hull.

Voice-over: The ocean currents are full of resources.

Scene: Glittering spirals of silvery fish seen from below the waves

Voice-over: Our factory ships are harvesting the microplastic particles of the Pacific garbage gyre and recycling them into . . . the uniform you wear!

Scene: Factory floor. Close-up of hands moving fabric while sewing buttonholes. Wide shot of smiling fabricators waving from where they sit at their machines. All wear AllMART uniforms.

Voice-over: Wear your uniform with pride. It represents AllMART's commitment to you, to our customers, to our planet.

Dawna Day uncovers a shopping cart full of uniforms. "Line up; let's get you all just what you need."

They don't actually have a polo shirt and pants in my size, so I end up with things that will probably be a little too large.

"You can change in the bathrooms. Hurry back! Something special will be waiting!" Dawna Day prods us along.

I'm hoping the special something might be lunch. I'm grateful for the bathroom break. It has been a long morning. While I'm waiting for my turn in the bathroom stall, I tear open the plastic envelope. My new clothes are shapeless. They smell like I imagine the ocean smells—like freshly washed garbage. But that must be my imagination.

The special surprise was not lunch. It was the head manager of the store, Mr. Middleman, come to admire us all in our uniforms while we sat at our desks. He waved from the door. That was it. Then we sat through another three hours of training vids.

I am exhausted. It's a longer day than any I ever spent in school, but it isn't just the time I've spent, it's that I'm too scared to relax. The desks, the vid screen, the way I'm learning—all of that is familiar—not scary at all. I'm scared because I'm not waiting for my real life to start; it's started.

I just want to walk out the door and go home.

That isn't an option.

"One last thing," says Dawna Day, my personal human-resources manager. "You all have a special relationship to

AllMART—certainly all AllMART employees are special, but *you* are extra special. You are now part of the AllMART family. It is part of a very ancient social contract, *in loco parentis*. This means that you are not employees. We are *family*. That is how much AllMART wants you to succeed—as much as a parent." The lights in the classroom dim, just a little, and her gentle voice says, very quietly, "Some of you may need AllMART very much. And AllMART is here for you. Some of you may be separated from your families for a little while. You may need a place to live, a home. It is very important that you know AllMART wants you to have a home. Each of you has received a text invitation." She pauses to touch the screen on her teaching device. "If you need anything, a place to stay, advice, or . . . anything . . . just reply to that text. We can give you the help you need. And it will always be strictly confidential. Just remember, that message is here, like open arms to hold you. Just remember." We all sit there, in the hushed and twilit room.

The lights get bright again. Dawna Day opens the door and says, "Give yourself a cheer!" We stand and *clapclapclap* while we file out, into the hall. Dawna Day throws her hands in the air and says, "We meet here again tomorrow. Smile, Belly! Let me see that special welcome mat, all of you."

I smile.

8

Timmer meets me just outside the employee exit. He is wearing his MORT badge and bouncing up and down on his toes.

"The 'Help' message sitting on your phone waiting for your reply: Delete that."

"Hello, MORT. It went fine. Thanks for asking."

"I'm serious. It's junk. You don't want AllMART to be your loco parents. Raoul explained it to me. I signed up, because . . . you know how it sounds like a good idea. But when Raoul found out, he flipped. He paid a guy to get it flushed out of the system. If you ask for that help, then they know they've got you. You get moved into the dormatoriums. Sometimes they move you away to work in the distribution centers—or who knows? Factories. It isn't up to you. It's up to them; they can move you wherever they want to in the system. You don't need AllMART to be your family. You have the Warren. Look, it's best if you just delete that message so it is never a temptation, but I get it if you can't do that yet. Just trust me. Before you ever reply to that, come to us; we are your family now. You need help, ask me. The deal is, though, you will help us. We know that. That's the deal." He pauses and turns his attention to his phone.

I can feel my own phone purring. I reach in my pocket and pull it out. WARREN has sent me a message:

The Warren is the only contact you need. Any trouble, send a message to the Warren.

"Just delete the AllMART Help message. Please . . ." Timmer looks at my badge. "ZERO! They did that to you? ZERO!"

"Could be worse."

"How much?"

"I could be beautiful BELLY."

"That happened?"

"It did, MORT. Did you ask? Is that how you knew it was a bad plan to badger the badger?"

"Me? No. I was going to wait till the end of the day, you know, be relaxed about it, not call out the mistake in front of an audience. It was a kid tagged DRAIN in my class. He said it was bullshit. It wasn't a human name. He got really angry."

"What happened?"

"Three days into training, he disappeared."

"You mean he quit?"

"He disappeared, like I said. Come on, it will look weird if we stand here. Follow me." MORTimmer walks away in what I'm pretty sure is the wrong direction. I run a couple steps to catch up.

"Look weird? Who's watching?" I say.

"The surveillance," he says.

"What surveillance?" I look around.

"Stop it. Don't look. Never surveil the surveillance. At least don't look like you are looking." He points directly ahead, toward a car far across the parking lot. "There are cameras on all the lot lights. Top of the posts. I said *don't look*! And there are drones. Mostly they focus on the traffic flow. But just know, they can always see you, so don't make yourself interesting."

I just want to go home. That isn't an option, so I just want to go to the Warren. If I were a dormitory employee, I'd probably be home by now. That really doesn't sound like a bad deal. I start across the parking lot. Timmer grabs my arm and pulls me in the wrong direction.

"Never walk directly toward the Warren. Always walk like you are going to the parking lot, to the bus stop or a car, then circle around."

"Why?"

"It's a Raoul rule. Purely precautionary."

We walk across the pavement. I can feel the heat through the soles of my shoes. Even though I haven't met him, I'm starting to really dislike Raoul.

When we open the door to the laundromat, 5er isn't the only one there.

"Hey," says Timmer.

"Hey," say the two people sitting on washing machines. They say it at the exact same time.

"Pineapple," says Timmer, pointing. "And Luck. They're twins." When Timmer says that word *twins*, their two heads bob up and down, synchronized, like they are bouncing on the same spring.

If Timmer hadn't said they were twins, I wouldn't have guessed it. Pineapple is bigger than Luck. Their hair isn't even the same color, but then, Pineapple's hair is an unnatural shade of red and Luck's hair is green, which is never, in any shade, natural on human beings. They are both wearing AllMART polo shirts.

"We brought ice cream—melted," says Luck, and hands a carton to Timmer, who tips it like a big mug and drinks from it. When he lowers it, he has a mess of cream on his lip.

"Want some?" Timmer holds the carton out to me.

"No, thank you," I say.

"You sure?" says Timmer. "It looks like ice cream is what's for dinner." He points at me and says, "This is ZERO. I found

84

her. She lives here now. Currently in training."

"I'm Zoë." I hold out my hand, but neither twin reaches out to me.

"Training? Look, if you want the coolest job, fail the tests," says Pineapple. "Prove you're back-of-the-store, behind-the-scenes material. Best chance to snag stuff, during loading and unloading. And you will develop mighty guns." Pineapple stops to display. Each bicep gets a kiss from its proud owner. Luck falls sideways laughing.

"Also, you can look however you want—even bored. Smiles not required," says Pineapple.

There is no way I'm ever going to fail a test, accidentally or on purpose.

"Who are you, really, Pineapple? What's your real name?"

"She's still kind of hung up on the name badge thing," says Timmer, pointing at me.

Luck sets down the ice cream carton and looks directly at me and says, "You didn't complain. . . ."

"No. She's safe," Timmer answers for me. "*Belly* beat her to it."

"Belly! Ouchy! That's almost as bad as Drain," says Luck.

"What's the story about Drain? You said he disappeared. What's that even mean?"

"It *means*," says Pineapple, "they took him, he's gone, and he isn't coming back."

At that moment, the dryers stop tumbling clothes. The air is hot and static.

Timmer takes a deep breath and says, "You need to know."

He looks at Luck and Pineapple where they sit, silent.

"Zero needs to know, right?" He doesn't wait for them to answer. "It's like this: Like I said, Drain was in my trainee class, and he got hotheaded when he saw his badge. He was ballistic about it. He wouldn't drop it.

"When I left that day, his sister, Soapy, was waiting by the employee exit door."

"Drain's sister, Soapy?" I need to be sure I heard that right.

Timmer nods and says, "Yeah, Soapy."

And I stop believing the story Timmer is telling me, right at that moment. *Soapy!* And *Drain!* I look around the laundromat and wonder if the next person in the story will be called Rinse—or Softener. I don't say anything, though, because I want to hear how it ends.

"The next morning, Soapy was there again, asking everyone if they had seen her brother. He hadn't shown up at all.

"People said maybe he just left. But Soapy said no to that. He didn't take the car, and that's where they were living mostly, to save on gas. All his clothes and shit were still in the backseat. He wouldn't have left everything. He wouldn't have left without saying good-bye.

"It was days and days, and Soapy still couldn't find Drain.

"She drove out to where they used to live when they had a whole family, but the place was empty. She asked all the olds who refused to leave the neighborhood. None of them had seen him. After that, she went to Dawna Day and asked to see the security camera data—she figured she could at least see where he went while he was on the premises, like which direction he went. Dawna Day said no to that; it would be an invasion of privacy. So, like I said, Drain disappeared."

"And that's it? That's the end of the story? What about Soapy? What happened to her?"

"Soapy is basically nuts," says Pineapple. "We see her sometimes because she works the back end. She's been permanently assigned stocking frozen foods during the grave-yard shift. Getting froze like that, it's usually a punishment for stealing food—you know, grazing in the produce department or swiping all the bakery samples. It isn't easy stealing frozen food...."

Luck holds an ice cream carton out like a trophy and says, "Unless you are really good."

"But," says Pineapple, "that isn't the point. The point is they had to move her out of customer service because she was always showing people Drain's picture and saying he was kidnapped."

"Kidnapped? That's horrible."

"You got no idea," says Pineapple. "Soapy believes AllMART kidnapped Drain."

"A week or so later, she said she saw him in a garbage gyre mining operation promo. But how could that be? It takes time to produce a polished ad," says Timmer.

"It's not like every product promo is made fresh. They just add enough new clips to keep it fresh. You know: 'Surprise is

87

the secret ingredient in memorable advertising.'" I'm quoting from Retail Psychology class. If Timmer recognizes the source, he doesn't acknowledge it.

"But why would he end up on a processing ship at sea?" says Luck.

"Yeah, that would be weird. Did she see him in a cheerful crowd scene? That's a lot of faces. Someone might have resembled him," I say.

"No, he was in the sewing room. She says she recognized his hands. *Pfft!* It's wishful thinking. She just wants to believe he's there, even though that place sucks—because the alternative is just not knowing at all," says Timmer.

"We have a psychological need for closure," I say. That's another quote from Retail Psychology. It explains the compulsion to watch a serial advertisement, especially if there is a narrative element. We all want to know the end of the story.

Timmer digs around in one of the desk drawers and pulls out a mess of keys.

"You need to see the places that are available, if you decide you really do want to have your own space."

I follow him. He's assuming that I'm going to stay. That's an assumption I still don't share. I'm considering other options. I understand the transportation problem, but I could ask Dawna Day for advice. I expect Timmer would have lots of reasons why that is a bad idea, but it isn't his decision.

I'm not sure he needs to know, and I may not tell him. Given the choice, I don't stir up a Dumpster full of raccoons. I feel the same way about arguing with Timmer.

Gravel grits under our shoes while we walk to the far end of the alley and stop at the door marked ERUPT SALON. "This is for Juliette," says Timmer.

"Pineapple and Luck have dibs on this one," Timmer says while we walk past another gray door. "They still go to their old neighborhood most times, or sleep in their car. Transitioning. It can take time."

I can't believe he is saying that to me. He isn't giving me any time for transitioning. I'm just supposed to move into this dead mall and live here happy as a roach in a soda cup.

"This one is available," says Timmer. He opens a door and I smell dirty carpet and bitter disappointment. Timmer flicks on the lights.

It's Jyll. And she's ready to sell, sell, sell a story of fun family togetherness. Except it isn't the living Jyll. It is a life-size cardboard Jyll, with a life-size cardboard smile full of life-size cardboard teeth. She stands behind an acrylic coffee table beside an uncomfortable couch. Jyll is holding a SOLD sign in her cardboard fingers. I am not sold. I step forward and punch Jyll in the cardboard nose and knock her flat.

"You want this place? You could sleep on the couch, I guess. I forgot there was a couch."

"No," I say.

We walk to the next gray metal door.

When I imagine sleeping in the back room of the fashion boutique where mannequin parts are stacked up like bones, my own bones wither.

"No," I say.

"This is your last choice," says Timmer. "It was an ice cream parlor, and then it was going to be a church, but . . ." He switches on the lights, and we are standing in an aquarium, a glass box full of buzzing, aluminum-flavored light.

"No," I say.

There are no more doors. Timmer answers my silence with silence, which is a good thing, because nothing he has to say interests me.

The sun has gone down. It is night, but the floodlights from the parking lots stain the sky dead-leaf yellow. Does the higher dark sparkle with disaster? Not that I can see. The promised satellite rain is invisible to me.

Just before he opens the door to the laundromat, Timmer turns to me and says, "Thing is. Thing is. Thing is: I don't like to leave 5er alone when he sleeps. He walks sometimes when he dreams. I'm afraid. I'm afraid he will just walk off." Timmer spreads his hands wide and empty, and I see what he means, all the wide and empty world and 5er invisible, lost in it.

Timmer is gone. He said he had stuff to do, but he did not elaborate.

5er is sitting on a washing machine with his arms wrapped around his legs. He is watching clothes tumbling behind a big dryer window. He spends the whole day here, in the Rub-a-Dub-Tub Laundry. The bright-colored clothes in the dryer flutter and leap, unkillable flowers in a merciless wind.

I lead 5er into the room where the mattress is on the floor. He doesn't resist.

"Go to sleep," I say.

He crawls into the center and curls himself into a wad.

"Do you want me to read to you?" AnnaMom used to read to me when I was little. I used to fall asleep to the sound of her voice.

5er doesn't say anything, but then, he never does.

I sit on the side of the mattress and reach into my AllMART bag and pull out the brittle paper book. I open it. It doesn't matter that I'm starting the story in the middle. All that matters is the sound of words. The words don't need to mean anything. I just turn the pages and read "And this disease was called The Loneliness, because when you saw your home town dwindle the size of your fist and then lemon-size and then pin-size and vanish in the fire-wake, you felt you had never been born, there was no town, you were nowhere, with space all around . . ."

I'm spending another night on a mattress in the office of a public laundry, too tired to sleep and too tired to look at the book in my hand. 5er writhes and makes strangled noises in his dreams. When I try to shush him, his eyes open and he looks right through me. He scrambles to his hands and knees, sweating. If he starts walking, do I try to stop him? Do I just follow him? Timmer didn't say. Suddenly, 5er's eyes shut and he goes limp and flops over, a hairless twitching kitten. I try not to touch him because touching him doesn't seem to help. I'm curled on my side into a question mark. I'm just one big question and I don't even know how to put it into words.

I pick up my phone. The screen wakes at the touch of my thumb. It knows me. It knows what I want. I imagine it circling out, higher and higher, calling out, calling out to find the shape of the world. Listening, listening for the love I need to hear.

She isn't going to call. I hear Timmer's voice in my mind, like he can suddenly talk to me whenever he wants, like his voice is the voice I need to listen to, even though it isn't the one I want to hear.

9

We play endless rounds of a game on our learning devices. The goal is to direct customers through the maze of aisles to a desired product, but extra life points are earned by interesting the customer in other products during the journey. This is made easier by little thought balloons that appear over the customer's head: "It's almost Mom's birthday; I'm thirsty; She's *hawt*!"

I touch the Special Occasion flowers, the supersize soakers in the drink cooler, and brush the endcap display of condoms as I thread my lucky customer through the aisles.

I am very good at this game. Of course, it will be harder with real customers, since their wants aren't written so obviously in the air, but there are always wants.

Wanting is only human. Humans are only wants. My purpose is to see tiny seeds of wanting that I can magnify and satisfy. Then, because I am human too, I will want stuff. The cycle is so beautiful. I will belong.

There is a test. A product appears on the vid screen at the front of the classroom. My task is to name it and give the range of aisles where it can be found. The items are difficult. Is this (a) a brown banana or (b) a plantain? I go with plantain, because this is a test and bananas are almost extinct. I use the same strategy to identify fresh squid entrails, tomatillos, and a ball-peen hammer. Once the vid screen wipes to black after the last item, it is only a second before our phones shiver.

"It's okay," says Dawna Day. "Go ahead and look. It's your test scores. AllMART family, I'm so happy to tell you that one of us has achieved a perfect score: one hundred items correctly identified and located. We all did great, but I know we agree that kind of performance deserves a reward."

I have at least two reactions to this announcement, simultaneously: I erupt in a shining moment of *Yes!* because for that moment it is possible that a reward is forthcoming; I collapse in a sunken moment of *No!* because the reward is almost certainly going to someone else.

The shining moment of *Yes!* happens.

"Collect your reward, Zero!" says Dawna Day.

She holds out a medium-size AllMART bag.

"Thank you," I say. Then I return to my seat.

"Zero, aren't you forgetting something? I'm sure everyone wants to share your happiness. Show us what's in the bag!"

Of course. I look in the bag. I've gotten very good at appearing happy, so I act like I'm unwrapping the best birthday present ever. I raise each item over my head in triumph and for the viewing pleasure of those less fortunate. "A ball-peen hammer! DentureTite! *Three* plantains! Kimchi candy! Can the whole class share the candy? I think there's enough for everyone."

There is more than enough.

Dawna Day says, "I'm proud of Zero. Zero has the kind of talent that is needed by the Retail Rescue Rangers. Haven't I told you about the Rescue Rangers? They are heroes. When there is an emergency, a commercial disaster, they are the first responders."

I'm not exactly sure what sort of situation qualifies as a commercial emergency, but that doesn't matter right now. What matters is that Dawna Day is proud of me. Dawna Day smiles, and I can feel it like sunbeams on my heart. It might also be the spicy-sweet heat of the candied kimchi. Either way is good. Either way my heart is warm.

"Plantains," says Timmer when I show him what I've earned. "If we had oil and a pan and a little sugar . . . so good."

"We can eat them without cooking," I say.

Timmer laughs. "No, I don't think so. But we can maybe use the chiminea. We used it to toast marshmallows. It worked okay for that."

It takes time to build a fire. It takes time for it to be hot. It takes time to figure out how to position the plantains so they will cook without falling into the coals. Plantains probably take a lot longer than marshmallows. And all that time, I'm hungry. At last, when the skin is charred, we decide we can eat.

We split them open.

"My Grammalita's plantains were delicious—crispy edges, a little sweet," says Timmer. "I would steal slices, and she would poke me with a fork, just a little. Then she would laugh and say, 'You eat them. You are a growing boy.'"

The food Timmer remembers and what we are going to eat have nothing in common.

"Wait," I say. I crush up the last piece of kimchi candy and sprinkle it on like salt. A little crunch, a little sweet; we all gather around and eat with our hands.

We sit around the chiminea long after the meal is through and the sky is growing dark. I look up. There is nothing to see; the stars and the satellites are all hidden behind the sulfur-yellow light of the parking lot lamps.

"When the satellite rain is over," I say, "AnnaMom will call."

"She isn't going to call," says Timmer. "It isn't because of satellite rain. If she wanted to call, she could pay to have it patched through the fiber optics. You know that. Satellite rain? You can believe that if you want to, but it isn't true."

10

It's a big day today. Today I graduate from classroom training to actual work on the store floor. I'm teamed with a supervisor and an experienced associate to ensure my success.

When I scan my tag, my phone trembles and I get my assignment.

TO: ZERO
FR: DAWNA DAY, Human Resources
RE: Work Assignment 1, JoyZone!
"Happiness is always on sale at JoyZone!"

DIRECTIONS:

1) Proceed to JoyZone! prep area.

2) Select costume. Note location of related products.

3) Watch product vid.

✔ BETTER KNOW A PRODUCT: DinoRoar TwinPac

Scene: A mother paws frantically through a bin of loose miniatures, holding up one plastic animal after another, while her son wails from the driver's seat of the KidMobileKart. She can't find the right dinosaur. The child's heart is broken; the mother's heart is breaking.

Scene: The KidMobileKart approaches. The mother stops at a tidy display, removes a DinoRoar TwinPac, hands it to the boy. Everyone is happy. Mission accomplished.

Voice-over: DinoRoar TwinPacs. Sure to please.

4) Report to Aisle 46 for your first day of work! Congratulations!

Panic flutters against my ribs. I don't know the way to the JoyZone! prep area. I'm going to be late because I'm going to be lost. Then my phone trembles. When I look, the tiny screen text says, "Take the corridor to your right, proceed through Inventory Stacks 37–46. Turn right at Inventory Stack 46. The prep area is on your left, beside the doors marked STORE FLOOR."

Now I need to choose a costume. Most departments have something to identify the employee as an expert—the camo vest for the Great Outdoors, for example. JoyZone! is a bit more elaborate because we are appealing to children and childlike customers, and their imaginations are—what did they say in Retail Psychology? Deeper and stickier? A seed of want planted in that deep, sticky brain grows like a magic bean. My costume choices are a duck bill, an elf hat, or a floor-length sparkle-power FairyPony Tale hair extension. Each of them comes with appropriate booties that slip on over my shoes. The duck bill is a flexible schnoz that is held over the nose and mouth with elastic bands. I can practically see the germs crawling around inside it from the associates who have worn it before. The elf hat looks promising but seems too seasonal. The elf footwear has long pointy toes with bells. I don't think I am ready to wear tinkling bells that might attract customer attention. The best choice for me is the glittery hair attachment and the high-heeled hooves that go with it. The hooves would be impossible to walk in if they were real shoes, but, as flexible plastic illusions, they work.

I check to make sure I know where these fine products are: FairyPony Tale toys, including SkyHooves, can be found on Aisle 49.

I will not, however, be working in that aisle. I head for Aisle 46, where I am to rendezvous with my coworkers. The air in JoyZone! smells heavily of plastic. The toys are off-gassing. I suppose people with children, and children themselves, are indifferent to stink.

The supervisor of JoyZone! is waiting, wearing a smile as big as a welcome mat and a pair of fleecy animal ears. She waves at me. Her ears waggle back and forth. "Thought controlled!" She brushes her hair up so I can see the silvery electrode attached to her forehead. "Found in electronics, not toys, boo!" Her giant smile becomes a pout, which is over and done in less than three seconds.

Then she touches her name tag and says proudly, "I'm DOLLY, Dolly Lamb."

My other coworker for the day approaches. The duck snout and rubbery yellow booties don't disguise the walk. I know that walk. It's Timmer. It is the first time I've seen him at work. Dolly Lamb bustles past me and throws her arms around him. "It's my *favorite Mort* in the whole wide world!" She pulls his face down to her level and plants a big smacking kiss on the duck mask. Then she turns to me and squints at my badge.

"Zero. Zero! It's your first time here, right?"

"Yes, ma'am."

"Don't ma'am me! I'm Dolly Lamb. We are all kids here, Zero. And. You. Look. *Adorable!* Swish that sparkly tail! Swish!"

I comply. It's kind of fun.

"Yay, Zero is a FairyPony. Okay! Today is dinosaur day." She points at a giant acrylic bin; inside it is a tangle of plastic animals, all different sizes and shapes. Outside? Sticky smears left by little hands and noses. "We need to destock these dinos! First, we sort all of these items into inventory buckets. Then we will install the new display brackets." Dolly pauses and squeezes Timmer's biceps. "We are so lucky to have these big muscles to help us!" Dolly seems a little lost in the moment. Her thought-controlled ears tremble. "Then we stock the space with DinoRoar TwinPacs. You watched the product vid? Right?"

"Yes."

"Of course you did. I hear such nice things about you, Zero."

She smiles. I smile. Our smiles duel; the biggest grin wins. My cheeks hurt. She wins. "Thank you, Dolly Lamb," I say. I wonder about what she might have heard. And I also wonder why it was so hard for her to read my name tag if she was expecting me, but those thoughts aren't happy thoughts. Those thoughts don't belong in JoyZone!

"Do you two know each other?"

I'm slow to answer, but Timmer quacks, "Yep! We carpool. We both live on Terra Incognita."

"That's dandy!" says Dolly Lamb. "How do you keep your hooves off Mort the munchable man muffin? I know I would eat him right up!"

Dolly Lamb's ears are vibrating again.

"Oh, we've known each other since we were little," says

101

Timmer. "We played together in the cul-de-sac—while we were still in diapers."

"My favorite Mort in diapers. How cute was that?"

"Kawaii," I say softly. "Perfectly *kawaii.*"

"I haven't heard that word in forevers!" squeals Dolly Lamb.

The three of us work cheerfully, emptying the free-roaming dinosaurs and sorting them into buckets.

"Oopsie!" says Dolly Lamb. "Almost put that one in the wrong bin. Can't have that happen. One bad dino can mess up the whole recycling process."

"These are all going to be recycled?"

"Yes! Recycling is the AllMART way. This little guy . . ." She pauses to wave a long-necked thing with flippers and jaws full of sharp teeth in the air. "He might become a shampoo bottle, and this"—she wiggles a frilled, three-horned, chubby one—"she could become a brassiere!"

This might explain why the bra I'm wearing is poking me. It remembers a previous life as a three-horned dinosaur.

Dolly Lamb's ears telegraph her thoughts. Happy focus, happy focus, happy focus, twitch to the back, droop. "Zero. We should be wearing hazard gloves. I'll get some."

I see—and smell—the problem. There is a bloated disposable diaper, size Super-Tot, in the dinosaur bin.

"You just sit tight. Don't touch a thing until I get back. I'll be back in two twitches of a lamb tail." This is funny because

Dolly turns around and wags her tail, a tuft of thought-controlled plush. Then she's off on her mission.

I stand there. I have a handful of dinosaurs I was going to sort into the buckets. Should I put them back in the bin? Should I go ahead and sort them? Am I being disobedient by touching them, even though I was already touching them?

"Z?" Timmer gets down on one knee and looks up at me. The duck mask maintains its cheerful composure. "Z, your bootie is crooked."

I reach and touch my backside automatically. How can my booty be crooked?

"Not *that* booty, that bootie," says Timmer. He points at my feet. One of my high-heeled-hoof booties is twisted off to one side. I bend over to fix it, but the dinosaurs in my hand make it awkward, as does the proximity to the duck. Before I can do anything, Timmer is adjusting it for me. But I also feel something pointy shoved into my sock. I frown. He turns his attention to my other foot. Something else is shoved into that sock. Then I see him stashing a bright green toy in his own bootie. He stands. He reaches into the bins and grabs another batch. We are both standing there with our hands full of dinosaurs when Dolly Lamb returns, carrying hazard gloves and a bottle of hand sanitizer. A janitorial services associate is following her with a scooper and an incinerator bag.

"Sillies! Go ahead and put those in the buckets," says Dolly Lamb. Then she squeezes sanitizer onto our upturned hands and models the proper hand-sanitizing motions with her gloved hands. We are gloved up, and the diaper is whisked away to the incinerator. Dolly Lamb hums a happy song while we work.

When that is done, the shelves will be rearranged to accommodate brackets for the plastic bubble packs of dinosaurs that guarantee happiness. DinoRoars are purple. They stand on their hind legs; their front legs can hold rudimentary tools, like bazookas included in the accessory bundle. They have small wings, which can be removed. The girl dinosaur has lovely, brushable hair in a mane down her neck. That's important. Her bazooka is pink. That's important too.

At the end of my shift, I unclip my FairyPony Tale hair extension and hang it back in its place. I smooth it out. I wish I could brush it, but I don't have the proper accessory to use. Then I sit to remove my high-heeled-hoof booties. That's when I can't avoid facing my situation.

I'm a thief, a shoplifter, a traitor to my AllMART family.

I have removed stocked items from the store floor. I am in possession of stolen property. The value—or lack of it—is irrelevant. This is a matter of principle. Right is right; wrong is wrong. I am in the wrong. I deserve job loss and jail time. I deserve to be sent to the frozen-food lockers with crazy Soapy and that girl who stole grapes.

I know that there are surveillance cameras in the changing room. There are cameras in the bathrooms too, so I can't even attempt to flush the tiny dinos down the toilet. I hunch over and hide as much as I can from the cameras I can't see but I know can always see me. I pretend I'm pulling my socks up, but I'm pushing the pointy plastic problems deeper.

Timmer sits down beside me on the bench. He moves the duck mask up onto his forehead. "So what do you think of Dolly?"

"She seems to love her work." I stare straight ahead.

"She is batshit crazy and stoned out of her gourd. She managed a slip-and-fall accident a couple of years ago. Now they keep her tanked to the gills, and she isn't allowed on ladders."

"Adorable," I say. It isn't my word. It's Dolly Lamb's.

"Well, come on. I'm your ride to Terra Incognita, aren't I?"

Slowly, like I'm tired after a long day of work, which I would be if I didn't have a gallon of adrenaline jumping through my heart, I stand and follow Timmer as he hangs up his duck mask and rubber booties. If the alarm sounds when I pass through the gate, there will be no arguing with the evidence. Dismissal, suspension, prosecution; a black mark that will follow me for the rest of my life; the doors to management closed forever: All because I am in possession of stolen recyclable trash I don't even want.

"Howdy," says Timmer. The gate security manager grunts, scans Timmer's tag, scans mine, and waves us through. Nothing. Silent nothing. Timmer holds the door open for me, and I walk through it.

* * *

105

"5er, we brought you presents."

Timmer pulls a dinosaur out of his sock and balances it on 5er's bony knee. "Z has some too," he says. "Look. They're cool, huh?"

I dig the toys out of my socks. 5er doesn't say anything. He just sits very still with the dinosaur balanced on his knobby knee. Timmer lines the toys up so it looks like they are all sitting watching television.

"This one is Raoul. Raoooul!" Timmer pretends the T. rex is roaring. "And this one is Juliette," he says, stroking a long, lovely plastic neck. "This is me with the horns, and that's Z." He points at the duck-faced one.

Why am I the duck-faced one? It seems like Timmer should be that one. He spent the day quacking like a duck, not me. And Juliette? Again? Who *is* Juliette?

"And this is you, 5er. This one can fly." Timmer lifts the dinosaur from 5er's knee and glides it to sit with the rest. 5er doesn't touch them.

I don't think anyone ever taught him how to play.

"I get why they didn't take you, Timmer, but why did they leave 5er with you?"

"What?"

"Your family, when they left. Why didn't they take 5er?"

"Oh, man, no. He's not . . . We're not . . . I *found* 5er, just like I found you. I pulled an inventory shift, and it went real long. It was way past midnight when I came out. I was planning

106

to go to Terra Incognita—like I did sometimes. Just driving home, you know, it felt normal. And I wanted to feel that. The parking lot was nearly deserted, except for the few cars in the far-awayest corners where people were trying to sleep.

"So I saw a pile of stuff on the curb by the exit ramp. I thought probly it was bag of garbage—but it coulda been useful, like a lost coat or something. So I was going to check it out. It might be useful. But when I started walking toward it, it moved. So I figured it was alive, a raccoon, maybe, or a small dog. I still thought, hey, check it out. I wouldn't get too close. What if it had rabies? And if it was a dog, though, and it wasn't bitey, it might appreciate a little petting—as long as it didn't have open sores or smell really bad.

"But when I went over close, I could see it wasn't a sick raccoon or a lonely puppy. It was a kid.

"Man, I think it woulda been easier to tame a rabid raccoon. I took me an hour to get him to say hi and tell me he was 5er. Then I had to sit there and ask a kajillion questions until I figured out he was waiting for his family. My butt was sore and cold from sitting on that curb, but I couldn't get that kid to budge. Damn! 5er was *rooted* to that cement. If I hadn't figured out the plan of leaving a sign for his family, we probly woulda been sitting in that sad place all night long. For the next week or so, he spent nights at the Warren and days on the curb, waiting. Then I argued him around to changing the sign so it tells them to come here if they want to find 5er. It's a nicer place to wait, and he can watch the lost and stolen child reports. Just in case."

"The lost and stolen child reports? Has he been reported? I mean by *you*? Shouldn't *you* report him to . . ." I was going to say the police, but then I thought about the black body armor and the invisible faces. "You could report him to AllMART security. They would know what to do."

"But we already know what to do," says Timmer. "We let him wait. That's what he needs. That's what he wants. He needs us to help him wait. His family didn't mean to leave him. It was an accident. They were traveling in four cars. One went East, one West, one North, and one South. The plan was to join up again when somebody found work. When that happens, 5er's family will all get together again. Somebody will count noses and notice he's gone. 5er just has to wait it out."

"Why doesn't he talk? I mean, if he told you that stuff about the four cars . . ." Suddenly I wonder if he did. Maybe Timmer just made this up, and none of it is the real story of that little boy we call 5er at all. Maybe 5er isn't even his name. "Why doesn't he talk now?"

Timmer shrugs. "What does he have to say? I mean, maybe talking makes it worse."

11

"How is it? Living in the dormatorium here?"

I'm working with Belly, stocking groceries and tidying shelves. It is not exciting work, but I like it better than working soft goods, where trainees like me always get stuck with the dressing room cleanup. At first I thought that little task was going to be easy: Just collect the clothes, put them neatly on the right kind of hanger, and wheel the rack full of tried-ons out to replace them on the floor.

That's not how it is.

It turns out that customers use the fitting rooms for toilets. It is much easier to get access to the fitting rooms than the public facilities. There is less of a line. Customers with urgent needs walk in, shut the door to the privacy-guaranteed changing room, and then walk out relieved. A shift in soft goods means suiting up in hazard gloves, scooping messes, and sanitizing surfaces. Janitorial visits once a day to mop up and wash away the graffiti smeared on the mirrors.

Soft goods is nasty, but stocking shelves with cans of fish products is boring and involves a lot of reaching and twisting. Talking makes work go faster, but Belly and I don't have many shared interests. She complained about the quality of the shopping music, which she says sucks. I explained that the music is carefully selected to increase the serotonin levels in the shoppers' brains, which makes them happier and more likely to linger and buy things. Belly said, "It still sucks!" Then she complained about how the new deodorant she bought is crumbly and smells like suck. Since I'm not in the market for deodorant at the moment, I just let that slide and shifted the subject to living in the AllMART trainee dorms. After all, Timmer's rabid commitment to living in an abandoned laundromat is based on loyalty to Raoul, not the actual quality of the living situation.

"It sucks," says Belly, but she says that about everything up to and including the free sample-size energy drink they handed us at the door this morning. She said that sucked and there wasn't enough of it in that "inky-dinky" bottle either.

I wait for her to elaborate. Even though there are two settings on Belly's world perspective — sucks and sucks infinity — she always explains. I'm learning from Belly.

"Living here sucks all of the sucking." Belly groans. "I have *zero* social life now. Sorry, Zero, no offense. The guys are all jerks, ugly jerks. We aren't allowed to go anywhere. It's straight from work to the dorms. We each have an inky-dinky bed and an even inkier-dinkier locker. Dinner comes out of the Eateria and there's no choice about it. We have to clean our own showers. During time off all there is to do is stare at a screen and sit on the couch. And we don't even get the good TV channels. And the only thing allowed through the spam filters is online classes at Unicorn. As if!"

It doesn't sound so terrible to me. That was what my life used to be like on Terra Incognita Circle: I went straight home after school. I ate food. I cleaned up after myself. I studied. I sat on the couch and stared at the screen. It didn't suck. I had my AnnaMom. It was wonderful.

The shelf in front of me is empty. It's supposed to be full of tuna cans, the small, flat cans of grated, packed-in-oil fish. I check the cart beside me, but there isn't product to replace it. I have several cartons of canned octopus, but the shelf space for canned octopus is full.

"Belly, I'm going to call for supervisor advice." I stare at the empty shelf.

"Why?"

"I don't have the right product—" There is a meaty, thunking *crash*, and my back is pelted with gobs of wet. When I turn around, there is Belly, on the floor, in a puddle of blood and green. The label on the broken glass says "Pickle Relish."

I touch my phone and the sound goes over the intercom:

"Emergency assistance Aisle 27, groceries. Cleanup on Aisle 27. Help! Please, help!"

"Were the two of you talking while you worked?" Human Resources Manager Dawna Day's hands hover over the tablet where she is compiling the accident report.

"Yes," I say. "I mean, a little. It makes the work go faster."

"What did you talk about?"

"It was work related." This is true, generally.

"Work related? Are you sure Belly didn't say anything else?"

I've already given her the best answer, but I can see she wants something different. "I asked Belly if she knew if the tuna girl custody case had been decided. I was stocking cans of tuna, and that made me think about it—the tuna-custody case," I say. "You know, the one on the news? I asked her if that poor girl's family had closure yet. It's such a sad story." I blink my eyes hard and a little tear squeezes out. Human Resources Dawna hands me a tissue. The conversation pauses.

"You are Belly's friend." Human Resources Dawna leans forward and tilts her head to one side. Her voice is tender but steady and targeted. Her voice is a nurse picking shards of glass out of a wound. "If she needs help, you need to tell me so I can get her the help she needs."

Human Resources Dawna pauses. The room is very quiet.

"Zoë, does Belly use drugs?"

"What? No."

"When I just talked to her she seemed very disoriented. Out of it. You know?"

"I think that was because of the jar that landed on her head. It was heavy. It knocked her down."

"But why did the jar fall? Could it be that Belly was careless? If she wasn't paying attention, maybe that's an indication that she might have been under the influence of something. . . ."

"It just fell off the top shelf and BOOM! There was no way she could have seen it coming. I mean, her attention was on the shelf she was stocking—the lower shelf."

"Did you *see* what happened?"

I think about my answer carefully before I speak. "No. I was working on the opposite shelf."

"So you couldn't have seen what happened."

"I know she was kneeling."

"You know what the saying here at AllMART is about accidents? Accidents don't just happen. Accidents happen because someone isn't doing her job correctly. Safety is everyone's job. The surveillance will show exactly what occurred."

I know the cameras don't pick up sound—just visuals. The record will show that we were working as I described. It will not reveal that I was probing Belly for information about life in the welcoming shelter of AllMART's dorms.

"But Zoë, never say 'Help' on the intercom. It confuses the customers. It makes them curious. They come to see what's happening, and that makes it harder for the First Aid responder

113

to do her work. Ask for cleanup. No one is ever curious about cleanup. I know it's hard to remember that in an emergency, so I'm just giving you a reminder this time, not a reprimand. Don't worry, Zoë. There are no black marks on your record."

"Thank you." I sound genuinely grateful because I am. I am genuinely grateful that this interview is over. I pause in the doorway as I leave to return to work. "Ma'am? What should I do with all the octopus? There is no room on the shelves for octopus. And I don't have the tuna to put in the empty spots."

Dawna Day looks up; that twitch across her face and intake of breath mean the question isn't welcome. She answers it anyway: "Just fill the empty places with the octopus. And strip the tuna price tabs off the shelf. We want to avoid confusing the customers. I'll tell marketing to push octopus."

"Yes, ma'am," I say. And then I go back to the aisle, which smells of pickle relish, and do exactly as I've been told.

My phone trembles.

It is set on work mode: I only receive alerts that pertain to work—and messages from WARREN—and AnnaMom, who will call. I get work-related messages all day long:

Take a moment to stretch!

Your smile . . . is AllMART's welcome mat.

Lunch break begins now and ends in 20 minutes.

Just a reminder: All public lavatories have been locked to prevent theft. Encourage customers to stop by the Porta-Comfy stations in the parking lot. Suggest they include a bottle of HandiHandsanitizer in today's purchasing.

Lunch break ends in five minutes. Are you ready to give your all for AllMART?

. . . and . . .

PAYDAY! Congratulations, your wages have been autodeposited in your account. Have a great day. Have an AllMART day.

I tap the link to my account, press my thumb to the screen, and enter my PIN: 1226. A to Z, Anna to Zoë.

I think I must have checked too soon. I don't have any money.

No. That isn't correct. I have *less* than no money. I am overdrawn. Even the little bit of lunch money I had left in my account when school ended is gone. That money didn't even cover the cost of my physical. Blood tests are expensive. I trained, and I worked, and I have nothing to show for it. No.

I have the debt I owe on my AllMART uniform. It cost a shocking lot.

When were still doing classroom training, we got some helpful budgeting advice from Pearl the Squirrel. She showed us how we could *$trrreeeetch!* our paychecks by shopping AllMART deals. Pearl bought nuts and berries, but only after comparison-shopping and checking to see if she had digital coupons. There was a real happy ending at the checkout stand. But Pearl the Squirrel is an animated cartoon animal. She doesn't wear clothes. That may explain why the cost of the shirt on my back wasn't included in the budget.

Meanwhile, I owe AllMART money. Then I think about compound interest.

I am not alone. Suddenly, short emphatic words punctuate the air above the shelving units and slither along the aisles. That passes, but I can hear a whispered weeping at the other side of the canned soups.

"I shoulda warned you about payday," says Timmer. "But even when you know how it is, it's a crap sandwich."

"How am I supposed to live on *nothing*?"

"Same as you have been," says Timmer. "Eventually, you will get money. I get money now, which is why we have delicious cereal." He shakes the box. "Just be glad you aren't living in the dormatorium. The kids in there will never stop being in debt to AllMART."

I think about Belly. When she complained about the

dorms, she complained about everything—except the rent. Maybe she didn't know. Maybe she thought she was living there free, like a squirrel in a tree. How much does an emergency ambulance cost? What about stitches? When Belly gets back from the SpeedyMed clinic, she is going to find that the dial on the suck-o-meter goes way beyond what she thought was infinity.

✔ BETTER KNOW A PRODUCT: Vote Bundling Services

Scene: A young woman is standing in line. Her attention is on her phone screen. Suddenly, it is almost out of power, and the line she's standing in reaches on and on; we see it from high above, coiling around and around.

Voice-over: Your right to vote is valuable . . . to us! Simply call us, Vote Bundling Services, and we will tell you how to turn your vote into something *you* want. Stop muddling with middlemen, faceless bureaucracy, and inconvenience. It's time democracy worked for you! Call Vote Bundling Services now!

Scene: We see the woman dial.

Young woman: Hello, Vote Bundling Services? (Smiles. Touches phone screen. Close shot of throbbing green dollar sign.)

117

Closing shot: She walks away, confident and energetic, looking fine.

Voice-over: Vote Bundling Services, because you know what you want – and we give it to you.

If I had a vote, I'd sell it. I won't have a vote to sell until my eighteenth birthday, and that's 619 days away.

≣ *CHANNEL 42* ≣

Chad Manley: **We have a breaking update on the Delores Perdita Cash tuna-custody case.**

Sallie Lee: **Does that poor family finally get closure?**

Chad Manley: **I know this story is important to all our viewers. Over to you, Sallie.**

Sallie Lee: **(Taps her teleprompter pad and reads.) Siftyfour and now it did depend report from all pataries has whole received for the hues of the garvens of today. (Her professional composure wrinkles.) What?**

Chad Manley: **Huhhuhhuh! I think you broke the story good, Sallie. Sanjay? (Chad touches his earpiece,**

118

nods.) Actually, the tuna-custody case is still frozen. The real story tonight comes to us from the campaign trail, where the Governor is rolling out a new jobs program.

Governor: Jobs. That's what people want and that's why they vote for me. A vote for me is a vote for jobs. Jobs. Job creators. Today we are here to cut the ribbon on a new facility, one that will provide jobs. And not just jobs — we are putting criminals to work. This empty, useless building . . . (The Governor waves.)

Hey, I know that building. It is Frederick Winslow Taylor High School, where I spent 2,942 hours in Room 2-B. I guess it is empty and useless now.

Governor: This waste government property is going to be put to use as a guano-mining facility. We — our corporate partner is Bats of Happiness — have already seeded in the colonies of bats that will be producing black gold. By next week, the facility will be fully staffed, putting prisoners to work as productive citizens.

Scene: The Governor steps forward with a pair of giant novelty scissors and cuts the giant novelty ribbon bow.

At the same time, the lids on large cardboard boxes are flipped open. The camera focuses on the top of a box. Nothing happens. A guy in overalls appears, grabs the box, and shakes it. Bats fly out. Everyone in the audience claps, except the Governor, who ducks and covers her hair with her hands. Suddenly the camera is flipped down. All it shows is the sidewalk in front of what used to be Room 2-B.

(Back in the studio.)

Chad Manley: Things can get rough out there on the campaign trail. Wow. Bats. What do you think about bats, Sallie?

I can see a black, flapping shape rise up from behind Sallie Lee's perfectly coiffed hair.

It jerks *smack!* right into her face.

Sallie Lee: I . . . (Screaming and flailing.)

Chad Manley: Don't be such a girl! It's just a toy. A bat-able squeaky bat. Available at Petlandia, AllMART! Show her it's just a toy, Sanjay. Back in a minute . . .

12

"This here is a matter of life or death." He waves his arms wide so I know he means his department, the Great Outdoors, Aisles 123–131. I put on my yes-sir-I'm-paying-attention-sir face and look around: shelves that reach to the metal rafter beams where the indoor sparrows nest, a taxidermied polar bear squishing a taxidermied seal, guns in glass display cases, guns on the wall. "Life or death. You get that, zombie?"

"Zoë, I'm Zoë," I say, and touch my name tag. It doesn't help much. My tag says ZERO. "You know how it is with the name tags, right, Karl?" I give him half a smile and a tilted-head shrug.

"I'm Kral. My momma named me Kral. You got that, zombie girl? And when I say zombie, I mean you're one of them that's not ready. You got you a bugout bag, zombie? You got you a bag that's got what you need to survive when it hits the fan?"

"Yeah. Yeah, I do." I'm not even lying.

"You got a secure shelter? Someplace to go when you can't go home?"

I think of the Warren. It isn't home, but it's shelter. "Yeah."

"You got food stores?"

I think about the wall of cereal boxes back at the Warren. "Yeah. We have food."

"The world is full of crazies."

I'm looking at one, but I'm not going to mention it.

"You got a gun?"

"No. But I've got friends."

"Unless they're friends with guns, they aren't friends."

I can see the gears shifting in Kral's head. I'm nothing but a trainee-employee so young I can't be bonded to handle money—even worse, I'm a gunless zombie. I'm worthless. And he is cursed with the thankless task of teaching me what I need to know to be useful in Aisles 123–131, the Great Outdoors, where it's a matter of life or death if somebody doesn't find the vacu-packed dehydrated celery.

At 9:45 p.m., the lights dim. Reducing the lights to 60 percent is a signal to the shoppers that they need to head for checkout. Their shopping day is over. By 10:30 the lights are down to 30 percent and the registers have been closed out and the lot wranglers are rattling long snakes made of carts with wobbling wheels home for the night. The store grows silent; the little sparrows close their wings and settle on the beams.

Kral calls me to the register station and inventory commterminal. With the main lights down, I notice that there are halogen beams focused on the handguns. I've seen that trick before, in the jewelry department: Sparkly, sparkly, don't you want me? Except here there is no sparkle. The beams of light are swallowed up by gun-shaped chunks of darkness. Then that's it. That light is gone forever.

"You did good today. You stayed busy." The praise is grudging, but I earned it. I scurried up the ladder to the top shelves like a squirrel. I sorted out the squid-body fishing lures from the flashers and the dodgers and never once gave in to the urge to pretend they were earrings. When consumers passed through, I made sure I directed them to our special sale item, the Red-E-2-Go emergency kit. When I took my ten-minute bathroom break, I was back in seven. If Kral wanted an excuse to bash me in the training eval, I didn't give him an obvious one. He starts to type, putting stuff into my permanent employment record. Then he stops and points to the stock cases behind him where the ammunition boxes are stacked behind lock and key. "You see how short the inventory is there?"

I do, and I wish I didn't. It looks like there's a lot of work to be done, filling the empty shelves, scanning the bar codes, and placing orders. I don't get paid for overtime—not during training. And I don't especially want to be stuck here, in the 30 percent gloom with a dead polar bear and Kral, doing unpaid after-hours work.

"We keep 'em short stocked," says Kral. "It improves sales. Heightens the perceived value. Know what I mean?"

"Yeah." I learned about short-stocking in Retail Psychology, but this is the first time a department supervisor at AllMART has suggested anything that deviated from the customer-happiness-comes-first AllMART way. Full shelves signal bounty and free choice, and empty shelves trigger anxiety and paranoia. That's classroom knowledge. I'm not in a classroom anymore. The customer psychology of purchasing ammunition may differ from the psychology of purchasing radishes.

"You take these." Kral hands me a stack of business cards:

AmmoRama
We got you covered.
@KRAL_NELSON

"Anybody asks you about ammunition, you give them one of these cards before you tell them Aisle 127. You write your name on the back so I know it was a referral. I'll make sure you get a fair taste."

I put the stack of cards in my pocket.

"Now, hop up on the counter over there."

I climb up. I'm almost eye to eye with the dead polar bear. I wonder, is that a real tongue behind those fangs? Or a plastic replacement? Is the polar bear a sort of mannequin, dressed in a fashionable winter-white coat?

"Little more that way," says Kral. I take a few steps in the direction he points.

"That's good," says Kral, and then he unlocks the gun case in front of him.

Crap. I must be in front of the surveillance camera. Kral's made me into a giant blind spot. He's going to steal from AllMART, and I'm going to help him. I stand exactly still and shut my eyes so I can be honest when I say I didn't see anything.

CRACK! CRACK! My eyes shock open. I freeze like a bunny.

"I hate them birds," says Kral. He's locking the case. The gun is back in its place under the glamour light.

"Think I got a couple. One's on the floor, but you better take the ladder and check on top of the high stock. They stink real bad after a couple of days."

I do as I'm told. The bird that landed on the top shelf is blown into bloody feathers and chunks, but I get as much as I can see and reach. My hands are full of bird parts when Kral calls up to me, "I'll give you a good review." Hearing that would have made me think it was worth it, but then he adds, "When it hits the fan, you come by my place and flash those zombie titties—maybe I'll let you in."

"I saw bras today that would hold wrecking balls, bras big as circus tents," Timmer says. "I spent the whole day untangling hangers and shoving bras onto racks. When I thought I was done, they just pointed me back to the beginning. There were bras all over the floor already, like winter was coming and bra racks were trees."

"I'm surprised they kept you late for that," I say.

"Oh, they let me go at eleven on the dot. I just had some stuff to do."

I think about what sort of stuff there is on Timmer's to-do list: rescuing damsels in distress, stealing gas, sniffing the wind, saving the world. I'm surprised he got done so fast.

"I worked with Kral in the Great Outdoors."

"Ah . . . Kral. Kral hates birds."

"Why didn't you warn me?"

"About what?"

"About Kral."

"Kral's harmless. As long as you aren't a bird."

"He called me a zombie."

"We're all zombies to Kral."

"He asked if I had a bugout bag. I told him I did."

"That probably impressed him."

"He wouldn't be impressed if he knew I was talking about a plastic bag full of old stories and underpants."

"Still, you are more prepared than most zombies, right?"

"For when it hits the fan." We both say it at exactly the same time, like it's a joke. It isn't a joke, but we giggle like raccoons anyway while we slink around the Dumpsters and through the parking lot toward the Warren.

126

≡ CHANNEL 42 ≡

Crawl: **"Breaking news! Special report! With Chad Manley and Sallie Lee!"**

Sallie Lee: **We have an important weather update.**

Chad Manley: **We have a haboob warning, folks.**

Sallie Lee: **The storm is approaching from the southwest. Wind gusts up to sixty miles per hour. Dust reducing visibility to zero. Everyone in the region is advised to find a safe place to park. Do not try to outrun the front. If you can see it, it is too close. And folks, this is a big one. Don't count on it being a ten- or thirty-minute storm. This will last longer than an hour. It's a gigantic haboob. Extremely dangerous.**

Chad Manley: **We all know how dangerous gigantic haboobs are. . . . (Wink.)**

(Quick zoom to Sallie Lee's décolletage.)

It's getting cold.

"It's bad," says Timmer. He is covered with dust. "I wanted to check on Pineapple and Luck, tell them it isn't a good night to sleep in the car. It's cold. And the wind is moving some big stuff around. There's all kinds of wrecks. Look!" He points at the front door. The world is dark and orange. If there are wrecks, I can't see them through dirt in the air. The lights flicker and dim. The television dies. The last dryer stops tumbling. All I can hear is the roar of the wind and the sound of distant thunder, or maybe crashing cars.

Some rain falls, drops as big as toads. The wind dies. Timmer showers in the dark.

In the morning, we go outside to look at the world after the storm. Smoke is still rising from some of the wrecks piled up on the freeway. Little dunes of driven sand have formed in the gutters. The chiminea is tipped over and the ashes of our fires have blown away.

The lights aren't on at AllMART. There are customers waiting for the doors to open, but I'm not sure they will. The electricity is still out. According to the Channel 42 emergency bulletin on my phone, it's a vast failure. The storm caused local outages, attempts to reroute power caused overloads, and the grid fried. It's feedback runaway, just like satellite rain.

When I enter through the employee door, there are black-uniformed special agents in charge. The Retail Rescue Rangers have arrived. Now I know what a commercial disaster looks like. I'm seeing one happening thanks to the Rescue Rangers' flashlights. Most human resources are being directed to the frozen-foods department. No power, no refrigeration. The entire frozen-foods inventory has to be scrapped.

We stand shoulder to shoulder, lifting soggy cartons and slippery plastic-covered gobs of meat.

The lights flicker and brighten.

The surveillance screens glow. The security cameras come online. The cooling units rumble back to life.

Three strong Rescue Rangers push a steel warehouse ladder into place at the front of the store. Dawna Day climbs to the top, even though that is a dangerous risk wearing such high heels.

"AllMART family," she says in a voice that carries. "In thirty minutes the front doors will open. And that isn't a minute too soon. There are customers out there who *need* stuff. And we are going to serve them. Because that's what we do. Haboob or no haboob. Power outage or no power outage. We do our part."

Right on cue, the AllMART jingle rings out through the aisles:

Each does a little part,
But all of us are AllMART.
clapclapclap clapclapclap, AllMART!
clapclapclap clapclapclap, Let's start!

We raise our hands in the air as one and cheer. A drop of cold blood trickles down my arm.

The cheer is over. We all bend back to work, throwing ruined meat into big wheeled trash bins.

As Dawna Day walks past, I can't help overhearing her private conversation on the phone. "Yes," I hear her say. "Things are orderly, and we will be open within the hour. . . . My opinion? . . . Middleman really isn't management material."

Rumors hatch and slither through the aisles: No gas for the backup generators. It was *his* responsibility. Was it stolen? Maybe *he* stole it. Middleman. Middleman. Middleman. We worked like dogs cleaning up his mess. And he didn't even show up. Middleman. The jerk.

13

"It won't make you happy," Timmer says.

"You don't know what makes me happy."

"True. I never saw you happy."

I don't even know what happy means anymore. Far as I know, it's just the physical reactions in my body caused by assuming the posture, doing the cheer, and smiling like a doormat. As soon as I scan out, I stop smiling. I'm not on the clock anymore.

"I just want to go home for one night. Please take me home. I know I can't stay. I get that, but I forgot some things—useful things."

"What useful things?"

I don't answer that because it is unanswerable. I'm not going to tell Timmer I forgot to bring tampons.

This morning, my phone background was a single pink rosebud. *See this, Zoëkins? When you see this flower, it means you need to be prepared.* That was what AnnaMom said when she installed the Rosie Reminder on my phone years ago. She didn't want me to be surprised and embarrassed. And I never was. When the pink flower opened its little rosebud mouth, I went straight to AnnaMom's bathroom and got supplies out of the monthly drawer.

But now the flower is yawning, and I am not prepared.

I could slide my name tag through the vending machine in the employee changing room, but the vending machine prices are premium prices—the sort of prices only a desperate person will pay. I do not want to be a desperate person digging myself deeper into debt one premium-priced cotton wad at a time.

I know Timmer has money in his pocket, but I'm not going to beg him for tampons. I'm just not.

So I want to go home.

Home.

When I get home, I want sleep in my own bed all alone. I want to touch the doorknob on my own door and shut it.

"You went back to Terra Incognita a bunch of times," I say. "I should get to go back at least once."

"And leave 5er alone through the night?"

I think about that, about 5er waking in the night,

scratching in the dark and touching only air, his strangled, gurgling screaming getting no answer, no shushing voice he doesn't hear but is there anyway.

"We could bring him with us. Why not?"

Timmer knows he's lost. After all, he used to leave 5er alone all the time, which makes him a worse person than I am. All I want to do is go back to my house and pick up some useful things. He turns his attention to 5er. "Hey, guy, we need to go for a little while. You should come with."

5er looks at Timmer and squints.

"I'll leave a note, so they know to wait until we get back." So Timmer does that. "We got 5er. Back on Thursday morning."

My house on Terra Incognita Circle still says FOR SALE.

The little strip of grass is smothered under the dirt carried by the haboob, but it was brown with thirst before the storm. The drought didn't kill the lilies, but they have been trampled and bitten down. I can see the heart-shaped tracks of deer in the dust. In the middle of the wreck, the last living petals on the last living flower on Terra Incognita are crumpling and collapsing. I pinch the wilting bud and crush it in my fist. Little things matter.

The front door is still locked. And there is junk mail in the box; not much—the profitability of direct-mail sales was finally not worth the trip—but collecting the Super! offers feels normal. I'm home.

I enter 1 - 2 - 2 - 6 A - 2 - Z into the security pad on the front door. It doesn't unlock.

"No electric. The lock was electric. You want me to break a window?" Timmer is yelling through the open car window.

"No!"

"What about the garage door? There's a door to the kitchen, right?"

"There's a passkey in the sprinkler box," I say. I kneel beside the step and open the box. The passkey is there, behind a spiderweb.

"You won't need that," says Timmer. He's walked up the sidewalk.

I step off the porch and go around the corner to where he is standing.

I can't pretend that everything is normal anymore.

The garage is ripped apart. The automatic door is gone; there is only an open wound with splinters around the edges. Behind it, the garage is a hole scattered with ruined and discarded things. AnnaMom always kept that space so tidy. It would kill her to see it like this.

I don't want to go in the garage. It looks so broken.

"Come with me?" I reach out to Timmer.

"I need to stay here where I can keep an eye on 5er. He's sleeping."

"Just stay close enough where you can see me too?"

"If there is a raccoon in there, don't mess with it," Timmer says.

"The kitchen door will probably be locked too," I say, but then I see that the wall between the kitchen and the garage is just another hole.

"The kitchen door, it's convenient access to plumbing," says Timmer. "The garage door is good scrap. These guys were efficient."

I am not prepared to appreciate the efficiency of the people who broke my house.

"Seen enough?"

I wish. What I can see through the hole into the kitchen should be plenty. Being efficient is destructive. The skin of the walls is ripped open, jagged tracks running where the electricity used to hide. The floor is covered with tufts of yellow fluff and broken glass.

"I'm going to my room."

"Be careful. I was serious about the raccoons. And watch for holes in the floor. And it still isn't a good idea," says Timmer.

Shattered dishes crunch under my feet. The living room isn't as ruined as the kitchen. There is less worth taking, less stuff worth breaking. The wire that was in the walls is gone, but the uncomfortable couch and the acrylic table are still there, positioned with psychological precision by Jyll the stager.

I climb the stairs slowly, pausing on each step to listen for raccoons and the aching sound I imagine the floor will make before it falls out from under me. *I love you twelve stair steps*, whispers imaginary AnnaMom.

The hall looks safe. It looks unchanged. I reach out and turn the knob on my bedroom door.

My bed has a new, fuzzy blanket of dust. Behind it, the wall is cracked wide open from the ceiling to the floor. I look out; there is nothing but wind between my eye and the sky. I shut my door and walk the few steps to AnnaMom's room.

The covers on her bed are wrinkled where Timmer slept. In every other way, it is ready to show, just the way Jyll insisted. The walls are smooth and perfect as an eggshell. Beyond, I can see myself in the bathroom mirror.

My phone hums. I see the pink rosebud, yawning. I swipe it away.

"Hey," says Timmer. "You okay? You . . ."

I thumb the phone to end the call. I can't have what I wanted. I can't sleep in my own bed, but I can have what I need. I go to AnnaMom's bathroom and open her tampon drawer.

There is a paper towel spread across the tampons. It has my name written on it—in eyeliner, the blackest kind, in curving brushstrokes. There is no doubt who wrote this: AnnaMom always writes my name with a little heart for the *o*, and she is very particular about the ¨ over the *e*.

When I lift the paper towel, I find it is a stack, all accordion-folded together. . . .

Z♥ë

I knew this day would come.

You don't need me anymore.

My baby is all grown up.

We are BOTH grown up now.

This is best.

+ make sure to renew your implant.

It makes things easier.

Anna

There is a yellow-and-black SpeedyMed label taped to the final towel with adhesive bandages.

I touch myself behind the ear. I'm not supposed to fuss with that hard little button, but there are times when I do, in the dark. If I push on it, it moves a little under the skin. If I push on it hard, it hurts. Its job is to make me feel better. That's what AnnaMom says. I should just leave it alone and let it make me feel better, but instead I scrape my nails across my skin and it hurts.

It's Timmer on the phone again. I don't answer.

I pull a pillow off the bed and shake it out of the case. Then I fill the case up with handfuls and handfuls of tampons. What else? What else do I need? Here's a tube of toothpaste.

137

I need that. Here's cotton balls, fluffy as bunny tails. Do I need them? I don't know. I don't know what I need. I just pull out the drawers and dump them. A box falls on the floor. It's open. I pick it up.

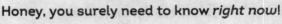

Buzzy Bee Early-Detection Pregnancy Tests
Earliest Detection
FIVE! Kits
Honey, you surely need to know *right now*!

There are three kits left in the box.

I drop them on the floor.

I don't need them.

I creep down the stairs, and over the broken glass, and into the garage. I can't see Timmer until I step outside. He's leaning against the hood of his car, staring at his phone.

"Hey!" I say. When he looks up, I drop the pillowcase full of useful things in the driveway and disappear back into the garage. I have one more thing to do.

I go to the cabinet where we kept the stuff for a barbecue AnnaMom promised we would have someday—when the weather was nicer or when she wasn't so tired. *We will have so much fun, ZeeZeeBee, but not today.* I find what I need behind a half-full bag of Bats of Happiness guano fertilizer, the kind that grows more beautiful flowers *naturally*. The can of lighter fluid is full. The box of long fireplace matches has never been opened.

I spray the uncomfortable couch until it is crisscrossed with dark stains. I leave a long dribbling trail to the kitchen door. That's where I light the match. It really is E-Z to Lite, just like it says. I throw the rest of the matches—loose—into the disaster that was our kitchen. Then I grab the pillowcase, run to the car, jerk the door open, climb in, and slam it behind. I'm not sure what to expect. Will the whole house explode?

5er lifts his head, shaky on his neck. I was noisy enough to wake him from his backseat sleep.

"What?" says Timmer when he gets behind the wheel and turns the key.

"Just go," I say. I think I can see a strange light in the windows behind the drawn shades. Pretty soon it will all burn down. The virgin towels in the bathroom will burn. The dresses I wore when I was Zoë Z. in Room 2-B will burn. All of Terra Incognita Circle will burn. That's what I want. When we reach the main arterial, I twist around in my seat and look behind me. There is smoke rising. It is very satisfying. This is how my face feels when my smile is my own.

Sunset comes while we're on the road. For a minute, everything glows like AnnaMom's favorite daylily, the one called Frilly Underpants. The sunlight's petals have ruffled edges where the sky touches the naked rock of the mountains. Then that is over, and we are driving under a gray sky on a gray road. Nobody says anything.

Not even when we get to the Warren.

5er is squatting like a hot frog in the middle of the backseat. He might be asleep. He is surely sweating. His eyes are
closed. Awake or asleep, he is peaceful. His drooping shoulders are rising and falling, just a little. He is breathing. He is
alive.

Timmer walks to the door and takes down the sign we left.
It isn't Thursday morning. It is still Wednesday. Then he opens
the car door, unbuckles 5er, and carries him, sweat and bones,
into the place we call home.

After Timmer is gone and 5er is asleep, I dig the paper towels
out of the bottom of the pillowcase. The black letters are blurred
now, smudged and rubbed when I crumpled the soft paper. The
prescription label is still stuck on at the end of the message.
I type the name of the medicine into my phone.

Need a consultation with Dr. Buzzy Bee?

Would you like to better know a SpeedyMed product?

Scan for product information now.

I hold the prescription code so my phone can read it.

Moody? Don't bee! Every day can be smooth and sweet
as honey.

What's in this little wonder?

Dr. Buzzy Bee holds up the implant. It looks like a stretched egg.

Better grades! Mood modulation! Happiness!

Inject this teeny-tiny implant under the skin . . .

I reach up and feel the place behind my ear where I get my implant renewed every year on my birthday. It's hardly even a little pinch when the insertion gun *Pops!*

    . . . and enjoy these benefits:
    • Better concentration!
    • Mood modulation!
    • Enhanced sexual responsibility!

I scroll down and down and down, until the print is tiny, tiny, tiny.

My implant is prescribed to reduce anxiety, oppositional behavior, and libido in girls.

I rub the place behind my ear until it hurts.

14

"Zoë?"

It is a very tender greeting, soft and personal.

I look up. My green hazard gloves are smeared and smelly. I'm sorry Dawna Day has to see this.

"Zoë, I came to see if you are okay. What happened is terrible. If you need anything, AllMART is here to help," says Dawna Day.

It is terrible when valued customers poop on the changing room floor.

"Maybe if this were just one large space it wouldn't happen so often," I say. I gesture at the mess. "Psychologically, I mean. It would discourage the behavior."

Dawna Day looks confused. So do I.

"I mean losing your home in the fire. I saw the news. That is your neighborhood, yes? Terra Incognita? Do you and your mother have a place to stay?"

I use the time it takes to bundle the mess into the incinerator bag to prepare my answer.

"Yes," I say. "Mom has an apartment for nights when she works late. It's a long commute to Terra Incognita."

"No need to worry, then," says Dawna Day. "I would like to meet your mother sometime. She must be very proud of you."

She turns to leave, but then she stops.

"Zoë, one last thing. When I looked at your file, I noticed you use medications."

"Oh. Yes."

"Well, don't forget to get your refill. Don't wait until too late to make the appointment."

"I won't forget. I've got a responsibility reminder on my phone. Thank you, though. I should go back to work now?"

"Yes. Yes. That's right, Zoë. Just go back to work."

Dawna Day's ring tone is the AllMART jingle. When I hear it, I have a strong impulse to jump to my feet, put my filthy hands in the air, and *clapclapclap*. I don't. I just focus on the mess on the floor.

"Tell Dolly Lamb I don't care if she refuses the severance package. She either resigns and takes it or she's fired and gets nothing, which is what she deserves. . . . Refill her prescription and push her out the door. . . . Fine! Tell her she can keep the damn thought-control ears. That woman doesn't have enough thought power to wipe her . . . Fine! I'll be there in a minute," says Dawna Day.

I look up and see her face. It is crumpled and hard, but when she looks away from her phone, when she sees me, she smiles.

"It isn't easy managing Human Resources, Zoë. They aren't all like you. I wish they were. And Zoë, that idea you had about changing the dressing room psychology. That's brilliant. I'm going to make sure corporate hears it."

"I had a visit from Dawna Day," I say.

I expect Timmer to say *Me too!* He doesn't. He just stops suddenly, halfway to nowhere in the parking lot.

"She wanted to know where I'm living now, since Terra Incognita burned."

"Where *are* you living?" Timmer says.

"My mom has an apartment for when she works late. We live there now."

"Good to know," says Timmer. "Remind me to never believe a thing you say, ever."

"Thank you," I say.

"I wonder where I'm living. Am I sleeping on your couch?"

"That would not be sexually responsible. I think you are living with your cousin Raoul."

He is still laughing when we get to the Warren.

* * *

144

After Timmer is gone, I read to 5er until he falls asleep.

I use pliers I find in the mop room—with narrow jaws and little grabbing teeth.

Voice-over: Needle-nose pliers are perfect tools for reaching into small places. AllMART customers may ask for long-nose, pinch-nose, or snip-nose pliers. If the customer uses one of those names, make certain to mirror their language in your own reply. Mirroring creates trust. Trust sells.

It hurts more than I expected. I can't just pluck it out. I have to tear a hole in my skin, which is difficult. But I always finish what I start. Or I think I do. Maybe I only finish what I start because my concentration is enhanced by the medicine. Maybe it's the little pellet under my skin that keeps me focused. Maybe it is what helps me ignore the hurt while I push and scratch until the job is done and the little rod spurts out, greasy with blood.

It can't help me focus and ignore pain anymore. I'm on my own.

I stand under the shower. My blood trickles thin, down my skin. I open my hand. My concentration, my modulation, my sexual responsibility: None of them amount to much. I hold my hand under the flow of the water, and when I bring it out, it is empty. I shampoo my hair in the smell of oranges and ginger. I scrub behind my ear with my pink-and-white-striped

145

washcloth; the traces of blood are almost invisible. It wasn't such a big deal. That's what I think while the remains of Zoëkins-ZeeZeeBee-the-best-student-in-Room-2-B swirl away down the drain.

There are Tasers behind my eyes, *zizzz-zaapp!*

"I'll stay with you," says Timmer. He sits on the edge of the mattress, reaches out with the back of his hand, and touches my forehead.

"No fever," he says. "I don't think you're sick."

I'm shaking. I've thrown up until I'm nothing but a crumpled, empty bag. It hurts to use my eyes.

"I mean, I don't think it's contagious. Did you eat something weird? Did you eat something we didn't?"

"No. No." There isn't any shape to that little word. Its edges are all melted off. It's just a ragged gust of air.

Timmer looks at his phone. "We have about six hours to get you through this. Then you've got to get up and go to work."

He stands and goes to the other room. He didn't stay after all. And the whole world is thick and sad. My thoughts are thick and sad. Even my tears are thick and sad. But then the pain comes back, and jagged glass crawls inside of me. It goes on forever, until Timmer comes back with my adventure towel, cool and damp, and wipes away the stale sweat and dried-up tears and the traces of puke off my lips.

When the time comes, he makes me stand up and shower. He buttons my pants for me. He lets me lean against him until we come to the employee entrance. Then he steps back, and I'm on my own.

Have I scanned this can of octopus? I keep losing track. Thoughts start, and then they stop. None of them get anywhere. My head aches. I pick a can of octopus up. I put the can of octopus down. I pick the can of octopus up again.

I touch the wounded place behind my ear.

I ruined everything.

I'm not good anymore.

I'm stupid.

Close your eyes, Zoëkins. Close your eyes and open your heart to sweet dreams. Imagine we are shopping, Zoë-baby. We walk up to the doors, and they are so shiny and clean we can see inside and see so many wonderful things, but then we open the door and walk in, and we are the only ones there. Now walk with me, Zoë, walk with me to the escalator, the escalator that goes down. We just stand and the escalator floats us down, like butterflies, through the beautiful colors and smells. And when we come to that level, the music is on but the lights are a little bit dim. It is very peaceful, and we are the only ones there. Then we go to the next escalator and we float down that one too. . . . And now the things are the best things ever. There is a ruby as big as my heart, it is shining on black velvet, and it is just for you, my Zoë-heart. Everything and all the best things are for you.

* * *

"Zero? Yeah. That octopus just isn't moving. People in this region won't eat octopus. So get a cart, pull it all off, and then spread the other stuff out. Sorry I had you count it first. It's all going to have to be counted again when they send it to the depot. So just stop with the inventory and pull it. Pull it all."

I am sick and stupid and slow for days.

No one notices.

ZERO finds the air to say, "May I help you?" *May*, because of course she *can*. ZERO can lead the way to the vacu-packed celery. ZERO can suggest the DinoRoar TwinPac is the best birthday present ever; and, if it's for a girl, ZERO points out that the DinoRoar Dream House sold separately is adorable. ZERO can and ZERO does. Her smile is AllMART's welcome mat; the fact that the face around it is puffy with tears doesn't change a thing.

15

I'm stretched out on the folding table, flat on my back with my eyes closed so I don't start counting the holes in the ceiling tiles. I've been counting things all day doing inventory; unless I force myself, I will continue and end up knowing exactly how many holes full of nothing are suspended over my head. Even with my eyes shut, I can feel it up there, the nothing. It is surprisingly heavy.

Jingle-ting! Clank-a-ding!

There is a shopkeeper's bell on the front door. This is the first time I've heard it ring. It's the first time anyone has opened that front door, which is always unlocked and waiting for 5er's family to come for him.

She is standing in the open door, tall and beautiful—so, so beautiful, though her face is grimed with slept-in, cried-in eyeliner. Tears are brimming up. They sparkle like broken glass.

"Are you here for 5er? Are you 5er's mom?"

5er looks up when I say his name, but there is no reunion. His attention returns to the sock he is twisting into a bunny for the hundredth time or five hundredth time.

"I need Raoul," the beautiful stranger says. "Is he here?"

"No." I don't elaborate, because I can't. The only thing I know about Raoul is that he isn't here.

"I'll wait," she says, and she sits down in one of the stiff orange plastic chairs. Her feet slide out of the sparkling slippers she is wearing. I recognize them. They were a special sale item last week. When they were gone, they left a gritty drift of glitter behind, a ghostly sparkle in the carpet of the shoe aisle. Janitorial vacuumed, but that only spread the glitter to other places. Today I saw it twinkle on the floor beside the duck decoys in the Great Outdoors.

She reaches down and rubs the arch of one foot, then she draws one knee up, wraps her arms around herself until she is folded like a wing without feathers. When she looks at me, I'm shot through with her need. I have no idea how to answer it.

I realize she is wearing an AllMART special-services smock. JULIETTE is embroidered in silver thread over her heart.

"Juliette? Juliette. I'm Zoë. How can I help you? Do you want a drink of water?"

She shakes her head no. She doesn't want water; she wants Raoul. I get the water anyway, because I have to do something. When I hold it out to her, she takes it from me and drinks small sips without ever taking the cup from her lips.

"You work at AllMART?"

"Yes," she says. It's a tiny little answer, and she says it into the cup. Then she straightens up and says, "I'm bonded and certified. I work registers and special-services departments."

She is not a family-hardship-waiver trainee. She is a real employee. She can count pills into the bright yellow-and-black bottles at the SpeedyMed pharmacy. She can pamper customers with spa footbaths full of nibble fish that kiss away flakes of skin and lavish crooked toes with attention like they were celebrities. She can sell lottery tickets at the service desk.

And she is still terribly sad.

I have no idea what else to do or say. The air is thick with nothing.

The back door opens, and we both look in that direction.

"Juliette!" The stranger is no stranger to Timmer. His voice bends with happiness when he says her name.

But she doesn't smile back.

"Juliette, what's wrong?" Timmer is on his knees in front of her. She droops down and onto his shoulder like a wilting flower.

"I need Raoul," she says to Timmer.

"Yeah," Timmer says, and he rocks back onto his heels. He grasps her hands, bites his lower lip, and shakes his head. "Yeah, he isn't back yet. This scrapping job, it's a big one—and far away."

"But I need him," she says. "We've been evicted."

"What?" says Timmer.

"I went home after work, and they'd thrown all our stuff out into the parking lot. Even the food out of the fridge. My card didn't work in the lock. There was this." She reaches into her back pocket and pulls out a folded sheet of paper.

"Shit," says Timmer. "Two months." His shoulders sag. I can see he's churning with this, trying to fix it.

"Raoul always paid the rent. He always said it wasn't my problem. I just thought . . ."

"Well, for now," says Timmer, "you have a place here. You know it."

She doesn't look happy.

"It's just for until Raoul gets back. Then he'll get a better place for the two of you."

"But I texted him, and he didn't even respond."

"Don't worry about that. It's just the satellite rain messing up the signals. Like they said on the news."

Timmer cuts a glance at me. He knows that I know that he doesn't believe what he just said.

"Come on, come on, Juliette," says Timmer. "We'll get you

152

all settled. Right, Z?" He points at me, and I put on a welcome mat smile. I don't know for sure what's going on, but something has hit the fan somewhere. And I know that beautiful Juliette is part of the family. She needs help. She asked for it. And we will help because that's the deal.

≡ *CHANNEL 42* ≡

Sallie Lee: . . . continuing our coverage of the fire tearing through the so-called dark neighborhoods. We now have Jyll Blotwin, spokeswoman for American Dream Homes, via satellite.

Scene: Split screen showing Sallie and Jyll, side by side.

Sallie Lee: Thank you for being with us.

Jyll Blotwin: Great to be here, Sallie. I appreciate the opportunity to reassure the viewers.

Scene: Distant view of burning houses in the dark. Then the screen is divided in thirds: the top stripe shows the top of Jyll's head; the middle stripe is a world on fire; the bottom stripe is Sallie Lee's boobs, held at professional attention by her business corset.

Jyll Blotwin: Those properties are all insured and secured. The fire is a tragedy. But shareholders in American Dream Homes should know their investment is safe. "Safe as houses!" Just like we promise.

Sallie Lee: Well, *I* feel better after talking to you.

Jyll Blotwin: Glad I helped.

Scene: Sallie Lee's face fills the screen.

Sallie Lee: The fire department describes the strategy as "watchful waiting." Rather than expending resources, they will monitor the affected areas with dronicopters. Travelers should expect traffic delays and reduced visibility due to blowing smoke.

Chad Manley: Now some information from our sponsor, American Dream Homes.

Sallie Lee: Was that supposed to be *funny*, Sanjay?

I think about Jyll. Much as I hate her, I have to give her credit. First, back in the days of younger, cardboard Jyll, she sold houses. But real estate agents only get a commission if there's a sale. The market shifted. There were way too many sellers and not enough buyers. So she adapted. She started staging houses, promising it would make the difference between SOLD! and sad-face emoji. Cool thing about staging: It's a service, and the service provider is paid even if there is no sale. But Jyll's best move was jumping to her position with American Dream, which put her in front of the cameras, explaining things to Sallie Lee.

I climb onto the mattress where I sleep and read and worry. 5er is curled into a ball no bigger than a pillow. I pick up the book from the bag. I stare at the ceiling. If I could see through the leak-stained ceiling tiles and tar roof, through the smoke of distant fires, past the glare of the parking lot, would I see the satellites sparkling as they fall?

My fingers smell like blood and feathers. I made it through another day. I spent half of it crying and half of it wishing I had claws like the taxidermied polar bear so I could scratch Kral's face right off his skull bone.

This is life without modulated moods.

Tomorrow I'm working in Petlandia. Will the little birds be frightened of the way I smell? No matter how much I try, I can't wash that smell away. I think it is inside me now, because it won't wash off no matter how much Ginger-Citrus BodiWash I use.

5er's small hands are curled around my shoulders. His bony knees poke my back. We can't sleep like spoons nestled in a drawer because he is so much littler than I am, so he clings to my hair and kicks me all night long. I wonder if he rides piggy-back into my dreams. I don't remember seeing him there, but then I don't remember dreaming, not since I started work. That's one good thing about working.

Another good thing about working? At least I know who I'm supposed to be, and I know what I'm supposed to do. When my shift is over and I step outside, when the hot parking lot wind touches my face, it seems possible that I might blow away, like a bit of litter or a butterfly.

16

Life isn't priceless. There are at least two departments at
AllMART where you can buy it: One is the Garden of Eden; the
other is Petlandia. Somehow, I never end up getting trained
to work in the Garden of Eden, although I want to very much.
AnnaMom and I always used to walk through there, even
when we didn't have money to buy a new potted orchid or the
need for more Bats of Happiness genuine guano fertilizer for
the daylilies. We walked through there because the air was
rich with water. The colors were brighter. It was hot in there
too, but that seemed okay. It was hot everywhere. I miss the
Garden of Eden. I miss the smell of plants and water. And I
miss being there with AnnaMom. But for some reason, I never

get assigned to work in that department. I think I would be good at it too.

Petlandia, though, today I'm assigned to Petlandia.

Most of the work involved in Petlandia has to do with sanitation. Every living product produces by-products that must be removed. Smelly by-products must not distract the potential shopper from the fun of shopping. Out of sight, out of mind, out of smelling distance: That's the ideal. There is a time and place for discussing by-products. That time is after the main sale is solid, after the consumer has fallen completely in love with the living product. Then comes the up-selling phase where the shopper is guided to buy the extra things they need. No kitten sale is complete without a bat-able squeaky bat: "It's a mouse with wings! It's kitten happiness!" No iguana should be sentenced to life without an Iguana-Logg: "Perfect for sun-bathing! (SunnyDaze sunlamp not included.)" And that's when the by-products matter. They should be mentioned delicately in the context of helping the shopper make additional purchases like an electric self-sweeping Kitteh-Kommode or a jumbo box of jungle-scented birdcage "carpets."

I never had a pet.

But I should be careful to use the correct vocabulary. We sell animal *companions* at Petlandia. Not pets: companions. That's what they said during training: It's an important philosophical distinction that matters to the consumer. I should always say "companions" even though the department sign says Petlandia. It will always say Petlandia because rebranding is costly and causes consumer anxiety. I think about the difference this way: I never had a companion except for AnnaMom, and she was surely not my pet.

Maybe, just maybe, I was hers.

Do you remember, AnnaMom, when I wanted a hamster dyed to look like a tiger for my birthday? But then my birthday came and I opened my presents and there were mittens that looked like tiger paws and a furry hat with tiger ears, but there wasn't any striped hamster. I cried and cried. And you said, "Look, Zoë-Zoë-ziger-cat. Look in the mirror. Look at your tiger ears! Kawaii! *Zoë-ziger." And maybe the hat was* kawaii, *maybe it was cute. But it wasn't a little living pet. It wasn't what I asked for so I yelled at you and said, "I can't love a hat!" And you said, "Enough now, Zoë. That's enough."*

But it wasn't enough. And I never ever wore that hat, not once. I wanted something to love, and a hat is not that. Never, never, never. But it's okay now, AnnaMom. I understand now. I know about the by-products and the extra work. I understand you didn't want me to learn too soon that love wears out too, faster than a hat. I understand how quickly pets wear out, faster than love. Working here in Petlandia has taught me the most unpleasant thing about working in a department that sells live products. They die.

Dead hermit crabs smell terrible.

Mother hamsters eat their babies.

* * *

No one buys rosy-red minnows or pinkie mice as companions. Those are food, live food for other animals. They will be consumed. This shopper must love her companion snake. This shopper must love his piranhas. I try to remember that, to respect that love, when I package those little slivers of fish, those hairless, shrimping mousies. I try to remember that and smile. My smile is AllMART's welcome mat.

"Zero, you can have an inventory shift tonight if you want."

What I want is to go home to the Warren and stand under the shower. The water will rinse the itch of litter off my skin and the waxy urine from under my fingernails. But it will not wash the ghost of Petlandia by-products out of my nose. So what I want is a shower and a nose that forgets all of this, but what I say is "Yes, thank you." And I smile because I'm supposed to be cheerful about extra hours. My smile is AllMART's welcome mat. Then, when I'm alone, I take a picture of the sign over Aisle 5 and send it to the Warren list. In a couple seconds, I get a photo of my underpants, twisted up into a flower, sitting like a hat on Pineapple's bright red hair. I don't have to worry about 5er. Pineapple has it covered. I just wish my underpants weren't involved.

Inventory is a little different in Petlandia. In Petlandia, the products move, and they don't have individual scanning codes. So inventory of the live products is sort of old-school. It requires counting. That isn't so hard with iguanas, which are large and slow, and it's sort of fun with the puppies and kittens. And Double Half-Moon Beta fish are easy because they sit on the shelf in separate plastic cups of water or they would fight to the death. But it is terribly difficult with the smaller birds, the finches in constant nervous motion, every one of them alike as numbers.

I know I'm not the only one. There are other trainees scooting like raccoons through the deserted, dim aisles. I hear the rumble of the ladder-stairs moving from place to place. Sometimes there is laughing or swearing. It depends on what that person finds during inventory. Along the top shelf of the Great Outdoors there are stray feathers and feet. Here in Petlandia, I find a little white mouse on a can of cat food.

"How did you get here, *kawaii* mousie?"

The mousie doesn't answer. It rubs a tiny pink paw along even tinier whiskers. It poops a tiny dark-brown rice grain of poop. I'm so in love. I even love the poop. I put my scan gun down and move my hands slowly. The little mousie doesn't run away even when I touch the top of its tiny round back with my fingertip. It lets me scoop it up and hold it in the hollow of my hands. I think it is also in the hollow of my heart. Kawaii *baby mousiekin, I'm your ZoëMom.*

"What are you doing, trainee ZERO?"

"Inventory. You assigned me."

"Inventory means scanning product codes. Where is your scanner?"

I nod at the cat food shelf. My scanner sits on top of the cans.

161

I smile and hold up my hands that embrace and make a little sphere, a little world, a little egg. I can feel the bright and busy feet and heart moving on my palm and fingers. "I found something."

She holds out her hand, I hover mine above, and the little speck of mousie is transferred.

"Damn popcorn mice!" she says. Then she flicks the little white life to the floor and steps on it. There is nothing but a smudge of damp meat.

"Look, when you find them, just kill them. Throwing them hard on the floor will do it with the bigger ones, but the popcorns, step on them or dump them straight into the incinerator. Those little suckers are hard to kill. They can't be returned to inventory once they escape the cages. Quality control. And these ones, the juveniles, they are escape artists. We don't sell them at this age because they are unmanageable. They climb and they jump. They jump so high they might as well be able to fly, I swear. A real pain in the ass. I mean, if a couple of them got to maturity, this whole store would be knee-deep in mice a week later—one consumer posts one photo of one mouse sitting on a cupcake in the bakery case and it's a disaster. So good for you for catching that thing. I'm glad you aren't squeamish or jumpy. You will be a real asset here in Petlandia. Make sure you sweep the turds onto the floor. Janitorial will be around in a couple of hours. If it happens on the day shift, call for cleanup-on-aisle."

At the end of my shift I pass by the fancy mice sleeping in Super-Savr Sanitary Shavings, pine scented. Tiny motions of their breathing in and out. Somewhere hidden inside is the tiny heart, a little wet unstoppable engine. That heart doesn't require any tiny mousie thoughts to command it. Like mine, it just keeps beating, even when forgotten.

When I get to the Warren, Pineapple and Luck want to play keep-away with my pink underpants. I'm too tired for that kind of fun. I'm too tired for any kind of fun. They give up and leave. I should take a shower, but I don't even have energy for that. I just stand there and stare at the screen.

✔ **BETTER KNOW A PRODUCT: Bats of Happiness Guano Fertilizer**

Voice-over: Bats of Happiness begins naturally.

Scene: A bat is born, hairless, with enormous, meaningless eyes closed shut.

Voice-over: For centuries people have understood the value of guano.

Scene: Sexy pirate with naked chest and poofy silk

sleeves strikes intrepid pose against the backdrop of the open sea.

Voice-over: Mining wealth found deep in the earth. Mining a renewable resource.

Scene: A trowel digs into the soil in a flower garden. The dirt looks rich and moist as chocolate cake.

Voice-over: We here at Bats of Happiness have a commitment to beauty and to life on this earth. We believe in managing resources. That's why we are seeding colonies of bats into abandoned factories, schools, and malls. Our specially trained bat-herds monitor their health and collect the valuable fertilizer.

Scene: Workers in red plastic coveralls walk through a cavernous factory. A hand in a red rubber glove holds an infant bat, feeding it with an eyedropper. A beautiful young girl bat-herd removes her protective hood and face shield and shakes her shining hair.

It's Belly. The beautiful bat-herd is Belly.

Voice-over: Steam-sanitized. Deodorized. Delivered to you.

Scene: We see bags on an assembly line swelling full of fertilizer and heat-sealed shut. The facility is super-clean, all bright white and stainless steel.

Scene: A flowering garden in an idyllic backyard. A bride and groom stand under a rose arbor.

CGI post-production: (1) Insert seven red cartoon bats of the product logo circling overhead; (2) Enhance color and number of roses.

Voice-over: Bats of Happiness. Committed to the future. Committed to beauty. Committed to your happiness.

I watch the entire cycle of news stories and product promos time after time. That bat-herd looks like Belly every fleeting moment she appears on screen, tossing her shining hair. And then the moment passes, and doubt and uncertainty make me sit and wait for it all to happen one more time. Next time I might know for certain. Next time there might be closure.

That is how Timmer finds me when he finally returns to the Warren after his late-night adventures.

17

There is a scratching at the door. I decide it is a raccoon.

Why would a raccoon want in at the door? Why would it persist in making the same *rattle-tap-scratch*? I look at 5er squatting on top of a washing machine, pulsing with the rhythm of the agitator. He doesn't need to know the answer to that question. I'm the adult. I'm the one who needs to know. It is my job. I walk through the mop room toward the back door.

Rattle-tap-scratch. I will open it just a crack and peek out—that's the plan. There might be rabies out there or . . . I don't know what else. But I'm ready to grab the big wooden-handled mop and fight. I'm ready to defend my home. I am ready to kill the rattle-tap-scratch. I'm afraid, but I'm ready. . . .

It's Juliette. She has her hands full. She is embracing two mannequin legs and a pale body. She holds a sharply jointed arm by the wrist. She pokes me with the plastic fingers. She holds a shopping bag in her teeth.

I reach out and take the handles.

"Little help?" says Juliette. She pecks out her lips and points at the ground behind her in the alley.

She's lost her head. It's sitting in the gravel. If it had eyes, it would be looking away, but it doesn't have eyes. It is smooth as an egg. That was the theory back in the day when this mannequin was cast: The silent salespeople don't need eyes; they don't need to see; they only need to be seen. Some mannequins didn't have heads at all, only necks that extended, unbowed, into nothing. I put the head in the shopping bag. It nests on crumpled tissue paper.

I know the rich history of the mannequin people. I studied it in school. The first were made of wax. They had realistic nipples and hair, real hair, fit strand by strand into their wax skin. Their eyes were glass, with mirrors set behind to give them a brightening glance. On hot days, they melted in the store windows and their red lips slid down their porcelain teeth like blood.

Those were the fierce ancestors of this vague blank-paper shell. Mannequins evolve, in our image, in the images of how we want to be.

"My keys are in my pocket," says Juliette. And she turns her hip toward me so I can see them, a disturbance in the curve.

She needs me. She needs me to reach into her pocket and pull out the keys. That's what she needs, so I do it. And when I do, my heart flips upside-down like a sad little refrigerator magnet. The reason I am touching her is almost jolted out of my head. I forget about her keys and her need and I'm only aware that I need something too. I want to be in her pocket. I want. I want. I want. I get why they are all so willing to carry her boxes and kill her spiders. If we weren't in the desert, Juliette would disorganize the tides.

Juliette shifts the burden in her arms, and I'm reminded of my purpose.

I have the keys. I lead the way to the door marked ERUPT SALON, unlock it, and brace it open while Juliette passes on a current of air that smells like peaches and toasted sesame.

The space inside the salon feels endless, but that is mostly because mirrors are reflecting mirrors in that hopeless, endless way that mirrors do. *no laSt purE*, the mirrors tell themselves while they reflect the mural of an erupting volcano and a painted sea with wooden boats.

"It felt lonely," says Juliette.

I look at the floor; it is scattered with arms and legs.

"Will you help me put them together?"

Yes. Yes. Yes, of course I will. And I will kill spiders for you, and I will do anything. I will live and die for you, Juliette, because when I put my hand in your pocket, my heart woke up in a whole new world.

We get 5er too, and he helps us fit the parts together as well as they will. There aren't enough heads. Joints jut in the wrong direction. This body has three legs and no arms. We have made them in our own image. The gold light paints the blank surfaces in glow.

I sit on the floor. 5er rests his head in my lap.

Juliette has stacks and stacks of tissue paper, all colors of the rainbow. It was wasting away in the dark corner of an abandoned stockroom until Juliette gathered it up and brought it into the light. I remember when shopgirls wrapped pretty new things in tissue paper cocoons sealed with special store stickers on them like kisses. I remember when I had an AnnaMom.

Juliette sees me crying. "You okay?"

I see her face is as wet as mine.

"Yes," I say. "You?"

She pulls her phone out of her pocket and shows me a screen. There is message after message from RAOUL. They all say "I <3 U." She scrolls and it seems like he loves her infinitely.

"Yes." And, though it is clearly a lie, we are both good with it.

Juliette's hands make magic little folds, and the pages of tissue paper blossom into perfect clothes for the Mannequin family. The floor of the store is covered with clouds of crumpled paper. It crushes and brushes around her feet.

She works for hours, while I watch her. Then, at last, she steps back, leans against a mirror, and says, "When Raoul comes . . ." The empty thought threads away like candle smoke.

18

Juliette is holding a baby on her lap. The baby, being a baby, hasn't learned that it shouldn't love Juliette with crazy abandon, so it does.

And Juliette, being Juliette, is loving the baby right back with the same crazy abandon.

It is a recipe for disaster.

"Just explain," says Timmer, "so I can figure this out. How come we got a baby?"

It's an excellent question. As we learned in Sexual Responsibility class, babies appear sort of slowly, with some indication like a rejection of bacon or a shameful shift in fashion awareness toward unconstricted shapes. None of that has gone on. We have all seen Juliette in her customary naked state. Seriously, she couldn't have sneaked this baby past us.

But still, there it is, with its wrists and ankles so fat it looks like it's some sort of balloon animal, a hand like a chubby starfish, touching Juliette's cheek while the drool of adoration shines all down the front of its grubby shirt.

"Thing is," says Juliette, "today I was working Baby Escape. I'm bonded, you know? So I can not only handle money and a cash register, I am authorized to work at Baby Escape, where shoppers hand me their babies so they can shop more conveniently.

"Baby Escape," Juliette continues. "It doesn't seem so bad from the customer side. Up front's the playroom, where there are always a couple of babies sitting on the cushy-colorful mats, and there's always as many staff as babies, helping them play with the toys featured in the JoyZone! sale-o-the-week. But there is also the back room, the nap room. In there, that's where we keep most of the babies who get dropped off. It's floor-to-ceiling baby crates. They got a door on the front, and they got a tray on the bottom lined with absorba-pads. And before we put the baby in there, we give it a shot of sleepy-time juice from a sippy cup. Most times, a baby is out for a couple hours before the family comes back. 'Shhhush!' we say. 'Baby's in the nap room. Come back in ten minutes.' They come back in a half hour or so, and we got the baby, all butt-clean in a fresh diaper, still sleeping off the sippy cup we gave them or, you know, a little subdued. And we say, 'She played herself right out. She really loved whatever-toy-is-featured.' And we point that out, and we scan the parent bracelet and we scan the bracelet on the baby's leg and cancel them both out of the system. If they buy the toy, there's no charge at checkout. If they don't buy the toy, then there's a service surcharge added to their credit card. Easy-peasy. Except this one's parent didn't come back.

"That's not supposed to happen. I wasn't trained for it. I mean, what was I supposed to do? Leave it there in the nap room? The morning crew would have noticed. And it would have been on me, you know? 'Cause I was the one who closed out the baby register at Baby Escape."

So there it is. The story of how we got us a baby. Timmer is staring at Juliette, and I can see his face is starting to soften. Juliette is cranked up to eleven, that's for sure. I know that baby was noticeably smelly when we walked into the salon and first saw it in Juliette's arms, a trickle of pink-stained curds slipping down its cheeks and disappearing into the wrinkles under its toothless chin. The bulging diaper, the spit-up—Juliette's wanting is canceling that all out.

"Timmer!" I say. "How are we going to solve this?" I need him to remember that this is a problem, not a miracle.

"Can you take it back in the morning?" says Timmer.

"I'm not scheduled to work at Baby Escape. I'm Fancy ManiPedis tomorrow," says Juliette.

"If the parents come back," says Timmer, "and they say 'Where's the baby?' What then?"

"I closed the register," says Juliette. "So that would be bad, I think."

"What was your plan?" Timmer has a lot of faith in Juliette.

"I didn't have a plan," says Juliette. "I just, you know, the lights were dimming and I had to do something."

I can almost see Juliette's powers of persuasion wrinkling the air like heat waves.

Tears collect and sparkle for a moment before they spill onto Juliette's cheekbones. "This is the sort of thing that will kill my chances for future employment," says Juliette.

"Poor baby," she says.

Timmer steps forward and bends to study the bar code band on the baby's leg.

"Maybe I can fix this," he says. "We know how the system works. We could maybe check it into the Baby Escape tomorrow? Pretend we are shoppers? . . . Who is off tomorrow? You, Pineapple, you work in the back so you're not so recognizable. You could pretend it's your baby and, you know, check it in . . . then it would be somebody else's problem."

I have a sick feeling. What if this has been going on for months? What if this baby was left there months ago, and each night somebody finds it and doesn't know what to do so they take it home and then they pose as a busy shopping parent?

"Well, shit," I say. "You can't just embezzle a baby. You can't just erase the transaction. Babies aren't fungible. You can't just swap them like wrong-size underpants.

"No," I say. "What we have to do is get this baby completely out of the system, permanently. For good."

"We can't keep it," says Timmer, but the way he holds the baby's round little foot in his hand, it is obvious he would like to find a way to make that work. And not just for Juliette's sake.

"We absolutely cannot! I'm not saying we keep it." How could that work? 5er is the only person home most days, and it worries me that we expect him to be responsible for himself, much less a baby. "No," I say. "We have to get rid of it."

They all look at me. I read confusion, sadness, a flicker of horror.

"Shhh! We're not going to smash it like it's an escaped popcorn mousie."

They hadn't thought of that. Now all the sadness is replaced by horror. There is still plenty of confusion.

"The SpeedyMed hospital," I say. "We cut the bracelet off and take it there. Sneak it in and leave it in a bathroom or something. I'm pretty sure they have surveillance in the hospitals, but we can work around that. I mean, we can scout the place out, stand so we block the cameras. I mean, it works for Kral; we can make it work.

"We can't spend time thinking about this," I say. "We just need to get it done. Timmer, get the car." I can't let anybody back out now. I know that. They know it too; that's why they do what I say.

By the time we get to the hospital, we have the whole

plan. It's a good plan. 5er and Timmer stay in the car with Juliette, because we all know she can't be any part of this. She is not a person who goes unnoticed, and I still don't trust her not to go wobbly. At least she thought far enough ahead to grab a clean diaper and some sleepy-sippy juice when she left work, so the thing shouldn't make noise or smell bad. I put the baby in my AllMART bag with some air holes punched in it.

All we have to do is go inside the emergency room, then Luck makes a blind spot, Pineapple starts a fight, I put the bag in a corner—and we all run. It is a great plan.

We didn't expect the metal detector at the doorway, but it doesn't matter because the baby isn't metal, so we sail right through. We didn't expect the really long line of sick people snaking back and forth in the hall either. But a crowd is good. Extra cover. Good. Luck moves into position and gives a little thumbs-up. Pineapple punches the guy in front of us in line. That guy turns around and snarls at Pineapple before he hits Pineapple in the teeth so hard I'm shocked. I'm frozen. But before Pineapple gets hit again, the guy is on the floor twitching and bucking. Tased. That's when we see the guard. The guard has already used his Taser, so he's got a gun drawn now, and it's pointed at Pineapple.

Luck is on Pineapple's side, though, and yells, "Gun! Gun!" The whole crowd stampedes and crushes against one another. We are close enough to the door that we get pushed back through the metal detector and into the street.

That's when I notice I'm still carrying the bag with the baby in it. Pineapple and Luck are running down the street. I don't know what else to do, so I put the bag full of baby down in the middle of the sidewalk, and then I run too.

I don't say anything except "Go, go, go" when I scramble into the front seat. I'm rocking back and forth like I can push the car forward with my own nervous weight. Timmer turns the key in the ignition and pulls away very prudently, which makes me nuts. I'm listening for sirens, which I hear, but there are always sirens in this neighborhood. Sirens are just background noise. I'm chewing on my lips and watching for I don't know what to descend on us, and catch us, and punish us. In the backseat, Pineapple and Luck are high-fiving. Juliette leans over and pulls Pineapple into an embrace. "Thank you," she says.

5er climbs between the seats and squats on my lap. He puts his hands on my cheeks and stares at me, hard.

"5er should be in a child-safety seat," I say.

"Seriously?" Luck says. "Shouldn't we all be in child-safety seats?" Everyone in the car except me thinks this is very funny.

We have turned eleven corners and idled at three stoplights before Timmer takes an on-ramp onto the freeway. That's when I say, "We are going the wrong way. We should be going east on Camino Campesino. This is northbound Enterprise Expressway."

"We did the right thing," says Timmer.

"But we are going the wrong way," I say.

"If we did the right thing, then we can't be going the wrong way. Trust me on this, Z."

In the backseat, Luck is wiping blood off Pineapple's mouth, and Pineapple is wiping tears off Juliette's cheeks.

"I miss Raoul," Juliette says, so softly. "I want him here," she says. And her loneliness crushes my heart.

"We did the right thing," says Timmer. "And so we are going to be rewarded." And we drive and drive, just like gasoline is free. Streetlights are still on in some of the neighborhoods we pass, but they become less and less common, until the places where people used to live are dark and dead as asphalt. And then even the dark neighborhoods are gone. There is nothing but the road and the empty desert night.

I want to do this forever, but Timmer takes an off-ramp marked THE VILLAGES AT MOONRISE RIVER MEADOWS. The developer must have paid extra for the supersize signage. When we come to the big iron curlicue gate that hangs between two tall fairy-tale-castle towers, Timmer off-roads around the obstacle.

The streets are all laid out and named with green-and-white street signs where they intersect with Moonrise River Lane: Anemone Avenue, Buttercup Boulevard, Clover Commercial Corners—we go through the whole alphabet until we come to Wildflower Way. There is a house on Wildflower Way, and it is the only house in the world, at least in the world we can see. All the rest of the lots are full of nothing.

Timmer stops the car and climbs out. I follow him across the sand and rabbitbrush toward the front door.

A little LED candle flickers on a windowsill all of a sudden, and a professionally trained voice says, "Welcome to Candlelight Cottage." Now the whole porch is bathed in golden light, and music is playing so softly I can hardly hear it with my ears. "Welcome home," says the perfect voice. "Welcome home."

"Go on," says Timmer. "The door is open."

I hesitate. "Welcome home," says the voice, as patient as only a recording can be. I guess I tripped a switch somehow, maybe when I shifted my weight from one foot to the other on the welcome mat. "Welcome home."

"It's all on solar panels. It all still works. You're going to love it."

In the entryway, there is a big flat screen, framed like a painting and showing us the very house we are standing in now, except it isn't stranded in the empty desert. It is where it is supposed to be, with trees all around. And it's magically wintertime, with a snowman in the yard. I can see the snowflakes drifting down like a dusting of powdered sugar on the tree branches and a rose arbor that isn't really outside. There is a smell of fir trees and peppermint. Then the snow melts away, and it is a sunny morning and all around the house there are yellow daffodils nodding and agreeing with the sun. While I'm distracted by the wings of a blue butterfly and a whiff of bread, the sky gets dark and suddenly it is full of blossoming fireworks. They are completely silent. They smell like vanilla. The sparks shower down, and all the leaves on the trees flare scarlet and yellow. There's a smiling jack-o'-lantern on the porch beside a basket of red, round apples. I can smell the apples.

"Come in; Candlelight Cottage is home," says the voice. The lamps start glowing, inviting us into the living space. There is one red chair by the CGI fire in the fireplace. A book is open on the seat. The carpet on the floor is soft and faintly colorless. The television screen wakes up and the camera pans around a room—no, *this* room—which seems more spacious filled with furniture than it does right now. This is how it will be: a bowl of popcorn on the table, soft pillows, an orchid, a mirror. And even though the view says I'm there, looking right into the video screen over the fireplace, I have no face. I am as empty as air.

"Why didn't they steal it?"

Timmer shrugs. "Dunno. I only found it by accident while I was lonely driving. Maybe nobody else knows. Or it isn't worth the gas and time. But you love it, don'tya?"

There is a sound of tinkling glasses to help the shifting lights guide us into the kitchen. "Made for entertaining. Made for family and friends," says the screen built into the refrigerator door. And it shows us how it will be: a birthday cake with candles . . .

But I stop watching. I reach for the faucet at the sink and turn it. Nothing happens. Timmer shrugs. The electric works because of the solar panels, but we are in the desert, and there is no work-around for water. Then he opens the fridge door. There's a piece of birthday cake inside. Timmer picks it up by the fork stuck in it, turns it upside down, and bangs the whole unit—cake, fork, frosting, plate—on the marble counter. Nothing happens. The cake is a lie, an acrylic fake.

We run upstairs, and there it is, the master suite. And the television there starts showing us how it will be, but all I can see is how it isn't. I open the door to the walk-in closet, and the smell in the air is of my own AnnaMom's perfume. It isn't fair. And it also isn't fair that there is a puddle of black silk dress on the floor and a pair of shoes, all like she just stepped out of them, and I should be able to hear her turn on the shower and she should call me: *Zoëkins, bring me a towel.*

"Come on," says Timmer. I point at the dress and shoes, but he isn't haunted by them. He picks them up, and they are only a trick like the cake, not real. He tosses them with a flip of the wrist and sails them across the bedroom.

"Come on. You hafta see the rest."

We cross the hall and open a door. The voice says, "Perfect for an office." And it shows us a gleaming desk, an executive chair . . . "Or a growing family." And the picture shifts and shows us a crib, with a rumpled blanket and a teddy bear but no baby.

Timmer pulls me farther down the hall. There is a glass door, and beyond it is a little balcony. "Look," says Timmer, and he points like he just invented the sky. Mars is rising pink and orange and huge over the eastern horizon. That's crazy.

I know it isn't Mars. It is only the moon, turned pink and pregnant as an apricot by the smoke from the burning world.

I can hear the downstairs rooms murmuring. Their stories leak out into the night. The empty concrete basements are quiet black wells, holes where the starlight falls in and is never seen again. I can feel all the rooms in all the houses that were never built, all the breathing of all the children who didn't live in them as they rock in the cradle of sleep without dreams.

19

I get up. I put on my uniform. I pin on my badge and I pin on my smile. I become Zero. It is a comfort, being Zero. Zero is working the first shift. Zero likes opening.

The lights are on, the music is on, and the doors are clean and shiny in the sunlight. The janitorials have made the floors shiny too. If Zero were a consumer, Zero would like to come early, before the doors are smudged, before the clothes are slipped off the hangers and fall to the floor, before the shopping carts full of products are abandoned by shoppers who remember they don't have money.

Zero would come to the store early. That's what Zero would do. Before every piece of fruit is touched and the bruises darken on the apricots and pears. It would be the sparkliest time, and Zero could move through the store as if it were all her own. It makes Zero feel drowsy and happy just to think about it.

There is a deer in the cereal aisle. At first I think I have self-comforted too much and I really have fallen asleep. Then I think it must be a special promotion—or a joke. Some joker has moved a taxidermied deer that belongs in the Great Outdoors to the grocery aisles. But then the deer startles. Its pointed feet tap and slide on the shiny floor, and its butt crashes into an endcap display of cereal boxes. The bright-colored cartons scatter across the floor.

I hear tapping and crashing and shouting and then a heavy bang. The sound of many voices. I walk in the direction of the noise. There is a crowd around the double sliding doors that lead to the Garden of Eden. When I'm close, I can see that the deer is there, on the pressure mat that opens the doors. The deer was going too fast for the doors to respond. Maybe it leapt and never touched the mat at all. It hit the shatterproof glass, and the glass didn't break. It is very strong glass, made strong enough to withstand an accidental ramming with a cart full of ornamental gravel.

Now, though, the door is hiccuping open from the dead weight.

"Cleanup at entrance to the Garden of Eden." I hear the announcement. "We open in five minutes, associates. Your smile is AllMART's welcome mat."

I look at the deer, so still. On the other side of the doors, I can see the plants, green and plush with water.

A janitorial services associate arrives pushing a mop in a wheeled bucket. The water in the bucket is fresh; big soap bubbles float on top. In a couple of hours, that water will be gray and smell like pickle juice and puke. He looks at the deer. He looks at his mop handle. Then he steps over the deer and enters the Garden of Eden. When he returns, he has a big wheeled cart, the kind they use for delivering bags of Bats of Happiness guano fertilizer to shoppers in waiting cars in the parking lot. He heaves the deer onto the cart and pushes it toward the nearest janitorial exit in the back of the store. He leaves the mop and bucket behind, but I see he will need it when he gets back. He will need it to wipe away the little trail of blood and filth that the deer is leaving behind.

The boxes scattered on the floor are waiting for me. It's a mess that I need to fix.

"Welcome to AllMART! It is a great day for shopping. A great day for you."

Five minutes ago, a live deer was dancing on cereal boxes. Now there is no trace that it ever existed.

Today, we are walking over the pedestrian bridge. Timmer has parked his car on the other side. When we walked across the bridge to work, both of us were silent. I was thinking about the baby, and how heavy it was inside that bag, and how hard my heart was beating when I ran away. But now, walking back,

Timmer reaches out and stops me. He leans close and says, "I have to tell you something, Z. I need you to know."

I can hardly hear him over the whine and gust of the traffic streaming by under our feet. I can smell his shoulder.

"You need to know." I can feel the breath of his words. "Raoul's dead."

This is not what I wanted Timmer to say.

"Raoul used to visit Juliette at work sometimes. Sure, AllMART policy discourages social visits, but Raoul was good at pretending to be a customer when anyone else was in earshot. It was hard for him to pretend he was a customer when Juliette was working in Fancy ManiPedis, though. Raoul was not the sort of man who got manicures. That he couldn't even pretend.

"So that day he looked for me, and he found me in the Garden of Eden.

"There was this big shipment of Bats of Happiness. I hadda move all these bags from a forklift and stack them in the right place on the aisle.

"I had a machete to use to cut the straps that tied the loads to the pallets, but it had to be done careful. If I got wild, I'da sliced a bag with the machete. That woulda meant inventory loss, and a cleanup-on-aisle, and probably some yelling at me for making a dumb mistake.

"So I was standing back and thinking about the best way to make the cuts.

"Suddenly Raoul was there and he made some joke about

185

the shit that makes people happy, and he slapped the load to make his point.

"The snake struck three times before I remembered I had a machete in my hand.

"I cut it in half, but it kept twisting and showing its teeth. It kept moving even after Raoul stopped.

"I tried that first aid thing we saw in training. But I wasn't sure how to do it. I'm pretty sure I was just beating on his dead heart. I started yelling, but no one came. Then I grabbed the service phone, and I could hear my own voice yelling, 'Help! Help! Help!'

"I didn't even tell them which aisle, so it took a while before they came.

"Then someone went and got a big wheeled cart, and they picked him up and took him away, out of sight in the back. Then a guy came and said I should come too. He took me to the back and told me to wait there. So I stood there by dead Raoul. After a while, I leaned over and hugged him.

"I know it's weird to hug a dead guy, but he was my friend. When I hugged him, his truck keys fell out of his pocket. I picked them up and put them in my pocket. Then I took his phone.

"It took a long time for the SpeedyMed ambulance to arrive, but it finally got there. They asked if he was family.

"I said no. I said the dead man was a stranger.

"I just stood there some more, after the ambulance took him away, until my phone rang and the message said to go back to work."

"I think Juliette should know. She needs to know the truth," I say.

"Promise me you won't . . ."

"It's not for me to tell. But you have to stop sending the texts. You can't keep sending her love messages from a dead man. The lie, it's making it worse. You just let her keep hoping Raoul is coming back, and there isn't any hope."

"There is hope. Months and months of hope. Raoul was gone before you came. He was gone before I found 5er. That's months of hope."

"She doesn't need hope. She needs closure."

"None of us ever get closure. Closure isn't even a thing, not really. I mean, I was there. I saw Raoul die, but it doesn't feel closed to me. When I shut my eyes, I can still see that moment, the time cut through like the snake chopped in half with a machete. Death opens things, and once they are opened, they can't be closed again.

"If I hadn't been there, if I hadn't seen him die, if I hadn't taken his phone and sent those messages, Raoul would still be dead. There would still be no way to fill the place in the world where he isn't anymore."

In the silence, the dryer growls on; my adventure towel comes and goes.

"Z, I told you because I needed to tell someone, and you were the only someone I could tell. You are the person I trust."

I look up at the television. I can't look at Timmer.

CHANNEL 42

Sallie Lee: . . . abandoned a baby—a baby!—on the sidewalk outside a SpeedyMed emergency room.

Scene: Footage from surveillance camera shows fleeing crowd. After the crowd disperses, there is a bag sitting in the middle of the sidewalk.

Sallie Lee: An innocent baby, left in a plastic bag, and that isn't the worst of it, you know, Chad? That baby had been drugged. Someone had given drugs to that baby.

Chad Manley: Who would waste drugs on a baby?

Sallie Lee: (Glares at Chad.) Let's roll that footage again. Viewers, please look closely. We are counting on you to give this baby closure. Somewhere out there this baby has a family.

Scene: Surveillance film plays on a loop.

There's the moment when the crowd parts and the bag is sitting there. By that time, I was running down the block, not even noticeable because so many other people were doing the same thing.

188

Timmer touches my shoulder. He looks at me, but he doesn't say anything. Timmer didn't know that the plan had gotten so messed up. He didn't know that I had failed to deposit the bag in the safety of the hospital bathroom. He knew stuff had gone down. Pineapple and Luck knew what they knew, which wasn't where I was and what I'd done before I showed up tugging on the car handle and yelling at Timmer to Go! Go! Go! But now he knows I failed at my part. I ditched the bag and ran. I'm not the one to trust.

Sallie Lee: Look at this baby's face. Can you help us bring this innocent baby home?

"The baby's safe," I say. "It's a celebrity. See?" I point at the screen showing Bag Baby surrounded by toys donated by AllMART, because AllMART takes a special interest in the poor thing. Pretty soon the news segment will get to the part where AllMART is going to feature Bag Baby in a series of public service advertisements promoting better parenting. The money will be invested in an account to make sure that Bag Baby has a great start in life.

"And we protected Juliette."

We stare at the clothes tumbling in the dryer. My adventure towel waves at me. A zipper clicks against the round glass window in the door.

The dryer stops. The clothes fall quiet.

20

When I get home from work, I watch myself on television while I take a shower under the sprinkler nozzle. I'm running away from the baby in a bag. That's what I do when I'm on the news.

Sallie Lee: Aside from this surveillance video, there is only one piece of evidence: the AllMART bag.

Chad Manley: The bag?

(Still of bag, spread on black background with a ruler beside it.)

There it is, my bag. There are many like it, but that one was mine. It held my book and underpants. I poked air holes in it with a pen so the baby could breathe. And I let it go.

Sallie Lee: Forensic analysis indicates that bag was manufactured almost *sixteen* years ago. If that bag were a human, it could have been that baby's mother.

Chad Manley: That wouldn't be sexually responsible. A mother who isn't even sixteen . . .

Sallie Lee: That's a tangent, Chad. The important thing is that there are *fingerprints* on that bag.

Chad Manley: Well, we know who did it, then! Evidence! Justice!

Sallie Lee: Not so fast. There are a *lot* of fingerprints, but only two sets are in the system.

Chad Manley: Sallie, you *tease*! Who done it?

Sallie Lee: Two names have been released to the public. I can share those now: Jean Brody, age fifty, unemployed public school teacher. Dolly Lamb, age forty-seven. Until recently she was an AllMART

employee in the — get this — *toy* department! Then she failed a routine drug test.

Chad Manley: The teacher. Case closed.

Sallie Lee: Not so fast, Chad. Brody died in an alcohol-related crash on the night of the big haboob. (Camera drops and focuses on Lee's décolletage for 1, 2, 3! seconds.) And Lamb was already incarcerated when the baby was dumped. Because she's a drug addict.

Chad Manley: Whoa! My money is still on the teacher.

I can't guess when Dolly Lamb touched that bag, but I know when Ms. Brody last held it. It was the day she gave it to me. My fingerprints are on there too. And Timmer's, because he carried it the day he brought me away from Terra Incognita. Juliette held that bag until we got to the drop zone. Maybe Luck's. Maybe Pineapple's. Maybe we are all there, waiting to be identified, but as far as I know, none of us has been arrested and none of us has ever taught school. Our fingerprints aren't in the database.

I take a deep breath. I feel safe — safe enough.

* * *

A message from SecurIt Safe-Keeping, to me and to 167 others: I'm about to delete it as old-style zombiespam, but my eye reads the first name on the list of other recipients and overrules that notion. The name is Jyll@magichomestaging.com. That's the same Jyll who taught me and AnnaMom how to live like ghosts. She is the one who promised that she understood the story of family fun and could tell it perfectly. She is the one who took my birthday pictures off the wall and put them in a gray storage bin somewhere. She is the one I hate. AnnaMom waved that little wave and left me behind with virgin towels and some Yummy Bunny leftovers in the refrigerator. I blame Jyll for that.

I open the message and read:

> The fee for rental on space 1226 is now six months in arrears. This is to inform you that the contents of Safe-Keeping space 1226, SecurIt Storage at 8700 Industrial Ave., will be auctioned on a date not earlier than May 4. This is the final notice that unclaimed items will be auctioned in lieu of rental fees owed. If you wish to claim the contents of storage space 1226, you may do so upon payment in full of fees owed.

I calculate the number of hours I will have to work to pay the total due: 383.$\overline{3}$. The auction date will come and go long before those future hours tick away.

"I need help."

Everyone looks up at me from where they are making s'mores around the chiminea—sort of. They are making s'mores s'more-or-less, which means they are smashing scorched marshmallows between slices of white bread. Timmer is squeezing hot sauce on his. I don't know if that is because he prefers it or if it is because it is possible.

"Really, I only need Timmer, but now that I think of it, it would be helpful if one of you hung out with 5er for a couple hours. We'll be back before he goes to sleep." I don't know if the others understand 5er's bad dreams, but I know I hit the right buttons to shut down a lot of Timmer's objections. "Can we talk?"

Timmer crams the rest of a slice of bread oozing burnt marshmallow and hot sauce into his mouth. He wipes his fingers on the back of his pants. "What?" he says.

I walk away a bit for privacy, then I turn and say, "I need a ride to 8700 Industrial Avenue. And I probably need some tools for breaking locks."

"You need to break locks?"

"Yeah. I'm going to bring my perfect-score-prize-reward ball-peen hammer, but maybe you know a better way. Like maybe Raoul has the right kind of tool, so we can borrow it from his truck."

"Raoul usually pulled the door off, you know, with a winch."

194

"Will that work if the door is inside a storage unit facility?"

"Don't think so, no. But I've gotta ask: Why are you interested in breaking locks all of a sudden?"

"I just need to get some stuff, my stuff. Personal stuff." Then I add, "Useful stuff," because that sounds more convincing than what AnnaMom is whispering in my head: *It's your nest egg, ZeeZeeBee.*

I'm banging on the hasp of the lock because I've decided that is the weak point of the system. Timmer holds his phone so I have light to see, and he leans hard against the metal door to deaden the noise. The light is little and the noise . . . the noise is the only result of my work so far.

"Ball. Peen. Hammers. Are. For. Working. On. Metal." Each time I hit the lock hasp with the hammer, I say one word: "Work. On. This."

A bouncing light. Someone is coming.

The place seemed deserted and unguarded. The electronic gate was open, since it was a dark neighborhood, so we just breezed right through and headed for Jyll's unit. It seemed deserted, but that approaching light means someone heard us. We're caught.

I grab Timmer's hand and press his phone screen against my soft body over my heart. That is how to hide a phone in a hurry: faster than fumbling for a switch, just bury the light. *Zoë-babykins? Are you sleeping? You should be sleeping. It is the middle of the night, and all the good girls are sleeping. All their phones are sleeping too. It must be a spark of starlight or a little glowworm I see flickering in the crack under your bedroom door.*

Hiding the phone doesn't matter. The heavy boot steps are still coming. The main passage is filled with the shaking beam of light. Barking coughs, the raking gurgle, "Little Zombie Titties! Whatcha doin', Zombie Titties?"

"Hi, Kral," says Timmer. He doesn't try to pull his hand away from where I'm holding it tight, but now I throw him away from me like it was his idea to be touching.

"Trouble with the lock?" says Kral. "I can fix that." He is only a step away from us. He lifts the heavy tool in his hand and pushes the long lopper handles together. The bladed jaws nip right through.

"Whatcha got in there?" Kral throws the lock. It clicks and skitters away into the shadows. Kral flips the handle and the door to the unit rumbles up. His headlamp shows me what he sees: stacks of gray storage bins. Kral reaches out and pulls one down, tipping the stuff inside to the floor.

All of us freeze. There's a snake. Kral drops his long-handled lopper and pulls out his gun and shoots it, three times. The sound echoes. The bullet fragments ricochet. Timmer turns and wraps his arms around me, curls around me, like that is going to protect me.

When the noise stops, Kral is snorting laughter. "The snake is a fake. Dead as a doorknob." He pushes it with the toe of his boot and scans the rest of the stuff that fell from the spilled bin: framed pictures of strangers, a flyswatter, a mug that says *World's Best Hookup.* "Junk!" he says. "You shoulda picked what's behind door number three, kids. Tell ya what, you come give me a hand, and I'll give you something worth the time." Kral turns and heads down the passage. Timmer follows. And I follow Timmer.

When the unit door rattles up, I recognize the logo on the packing. The unit is full pretty much top to bottom with boxes of ammunition.

"I need to load this up," says Kral. "Got me a hand truck, but now I got me some hands."

Timmer doesn't say anything. He just starts loading the boxes onto the hand truck while Kral supervises. Or maybe Kral is just making sure Timmer has light to see by. When it's full, Kral and Timmer head off down the passage, and I'm left there, in the dark.

It seems like a very long time before I see the jumping light and I hear them coming back. Them. Both of them. Timmer and Kral.

"This is going to take a while," says Timmer. He hands me his phone. "You can use this to look for your stuff."

"Okay, but I can use my own phone. You keep yours."

I wait until Timmer has filled the hand truck with another load of ammunition and they leave me alone in the dark again. Then I touch my phone and hold it out so it can make its small light in the dark place.

* * *

197

Jyll's Safe-Keeping unit is larger than Kral's. Toward the back there is a stack of crystal-clear coffee tables and a rack to hold large artwork. I recognize the frame of the painting that used to hang over the fireplace in my home in Terra Incognita. I pull it out and lean it against the stack of tables. I have seen this every day for most of my life. Or I could have seen it, if I had looked at it. I haven't looked at it for a long time. That's the way it can be with familiar objects.

It is a painting about Africa. The sky is full of storm clouds, blue so dark it has turned black. The earth is tender yellow green. Six white birds fly overhead, because they can fly. The ostrich, which is what the painting is really about, cannot. It is posed on one foot; the other leg is lifted in the air like a ballerina's. White plumes frill out in a tutu. The bird's neck curves gracefully. It has long eyelashes and enormous eyes. It is the eyes that terrify me, black and empty and bottomless.

Or those painted eyes did terrify me when I was little. If I am terrified now, I can't tell. I live in fear. I am a chick in an egg, and fear is the slippery, clear goo around me. I stand eye to eye with the ostrich, and my heart, that stubborn muscle, just keeps hammering on inside me like it wants to escape.

Jyll was big on organization. Jyll was proud of her skills. So I know everything in this unit is in a logical place; I'm just not sure what logic Jyll was using. The gray bins are labeled, but they aren't addresses, just numbers. It takes me a while to figure out the numbers are dates. Some of the bins have been in the unit for more than four years. Our bin has been stored and waiting for nine months.

Here is the genuine ostrich feather plume, framed. The repainted china plate where the ostrich looks up from a circle of old-fashioned roses. There are the framed pictures of me, each year on my birthday, and in each photo I have the photos from the year before until the last one, where it is me, sitting at the kitchen island, with fourteen frames and a piece of special cake from the Casa de Cake Haus. And, wrapped in bubble wrap for safekeeping, the big egg that can be filled with water and buried in the sand of the desert . . . *because water in the desert is like a treasure once-upon-a-time, Zoëkins. Kiss it! Kiss it, ZeeZeeBee. We can fill it up with love just in case we ever need it, just in case we are ever in the desert and we need to drink up some love.*

I can't stop the tear. It falls right into the hole on the top and disappears. The egg only pretends to be safekeeping. It isn't a bank for kisses. The weight of a tear, the weight of all those kisses, amounts to nothing. When I hold the shell, it only feels empty.

ZeeZeeBee, don't you cry. Girls like us, we don't cry. I love you and you love me. . . .

"Shut up! Shut up! Shut up!" It's a wonder the egg doesn't crush in my hands. My fingers are turning into claws. The egg holds firm. I lift it over my head and throw it—spike it— right against the cement floor of the storage unit. That's when it cracks. I stomp on it. It crunches like broken china bowls. I stomp on it a lot.

When I look, I see the broken shell, dry as bone, the color of bone. And I see something else.

It's a photograph, printed out on shiny paper, suitable for framing, like my birthday pictures. It's a guy with a little girl riding on his shoulders. The guy and the little girl are both smiling. I turn the curled paper over. "Ed and ZeeZeeBee." It is my mother's precise handwriting. There is a date too, printed by the photo shop in pale blue ink and diagonal lines. Funny thing, it is dated my own birthday, when I would have been three years old. I can't remember being three. I mean, I can't remember anything about being three that my AnnaMom didn't tell me with the pictures she showed me. She never showed me this picture. I do know that Ed Gorton, who is the only Ed I know about, was already dead by ostrich a long time before my third birthday.

I see light bouncing in the dark hallway. I put the photo in my back pocket.

"You find what you needed?" asks Timmer. I look past him. Kral doesn't seem to be with him.

I pick up my tiny, tarnished silver spoon. "I found this."

"That's something," says Timmer. "Do you need to look some more?"

"No. I'm done."

"Kral gave us this," says Timmer, and he points to the headlamp he's wearing. "And this too," he says. He reaches around his back and then holds out a gun, small and dark. It's

200

an inexpensive but popular model. It is the darkest thing in that lightless place. "Ammo included," Timmer says. Then he pauses and looks up at me. The headlamp blinds me when he stares at my face. "Kral says he's willing to take you if you want to go with him. He'll wait for fifteen minutes. Kral always liked you."

"No," I say. "He can wait all night."

"Okay."

"Shut the door, please," I say.

Timmer turns, reaches up, and pulls the rattling metal panels of the storage unit door down.

"All the way," I say.

"Sorry, it got hung up on this tub that spilled," Timmer says. He moves to pick up the overturned bin.

"No! Don't touch it. The snake is under there."

"The snake is a lie. It can't bite," says Timmer.

"Just shut up and turn off that light."

"Then we will be in the dark."

"Shut up and shut it off."

The light goes off. There is that sudden feeling of my eyes opening desperately and looking so deep that I can feel the gaze sliding back into me. It sneaks up invisible and swallows itself.

In the dark, blind fingers resort to reaching out. Which is why Timmer touches my nose but then jerks back, because it's very . . . it's socially unheard-of to walk up and touch someone on the nose.

Even on Mars, they shake hands instead of that.

Then Timmer is actually close to me and he puts his arms around me and hugs me. His shirt is damp from the work he did for Kral. The signal for hug:ended never happens. I'm surprised how his bones stick out. I am surprised by his body. I am surprised by the sound of my silver spoon ringing on the floor when I open my clenched fist.

21

Now that Kral is gone, I'm promoted to full-time counter manager at the Great Outdoors. I am handling the department all by myself and doing all the work that Kral used to do. Except I don't shoot birds after hours—and I'm still not of age to be bonded, so I can't cash register. But I am entrusted with the keys to the ammo and display cases. I am trusted to help customers make the choice that is best for their needs, although most customers know exactly what they want and don't even look at me while I just hand it over and smile. Whether they see it or not, my smile is AllMART's welcome mat.

But today I have a customer who doesn't know what she wants. She stands by the glass display cases and taps her nails on the surface. They are beautiful nails; each of them is like a little lens that catches the light and bounces it back, a flash of violet, a flash of rose. Her fingertips are iridescent twinkles. I will ask Juliette if she knows about those kinds of nails.

"How can I help you?" I remember to smile when I ask, because the voice changes when a person smiles. A smile can be heard over the phone. People know what sort of person you are as soon as you say hello. It is a moment of trust. There is no changing that first impression. If the sale is to be made, I must sell myself. That is the research. And now I do these things without thinking about them. I am a fully trained employee.

"I need a gun," the customer says. She stops tapping the glass and grasps her arms across her body. "Which one is good?"

"All our guns are excellent. Is this a gift?" I am going to tell her about our special gift card offer and how that lets that special someone enjoy the shopping experience, but her body contracts as she flinches back from the counter. A grimace flickers across her face. I'm afraid I might have lost the sale. But then she lifts her chin, and says, "It's for me."

"Excellent. A handgun, then, not a rifle?" I smile while I unlock the case. She says nothing, which means that I am correct. I take out a small gun. It is pink.

She has lovely eyelashes; they have extensions that look like vines and butterflies. Beautiful, she is beautiful. But there is a little too much concealer under one eye. And one of her fingernails is missing—replaced with a stretchy transparent bandage stained brown with old blood.

Her face is familiar, but I am careful not to say anything about that. It is important to respect the customer's privacy. This is especially true of beautiful customers. There is a tendency to desire intimacy with them, to confuse the recognition of beauty with familiarity, to presume they find us attractive too. I don't give in to any of that. I am perfectly professional.

"Is this a good gun?"

"It is great! And so *kawaii*! It will fit in a small purse. Adorable!" I'm smiling as I say the words.

"But is it strong? Is it as strong as those?" She points at the other guns in the case. The black ones.

"Yes! Absolutely. It is just as strong as that gun right there. They are the same model. The same in every way. Except this one is pink! So *kawaii*!"

She goes back to tapping on the glass with her fingernails. She pushes the gun with one finger. It spins on the surface, one slow rotation and a little bit more.

"You will also need ammunition." I turn and select the right caliber and place it beside the gun.

"Okay," the customer says. She reaches out and pushes the gun again with her finger. Again it spins slowly and comes to a stop.

"It comes with a free trigger lock, because AllMART cares about our customers."

"Okay," the customer says.

"I'm sorry that our shooting range is closed for remodeling," I say. Of course it isn't being remodeled. It is temporarily closed because there is no associate to provide skilled instruction and advice. We are shorthanded because Kral isn't the only employee to take advantage of the generous severance package for those employed more than three years who are eager for new opportunities. But telling that truth would not enhance the shopping experience for this customer. The story that the service is closed for remodeling helps her focus on a future where her AllMART visits will be better and better, new and improved.

"Can you take this thing out?" She taps the trigger lock.

"That is handled at the courtesy desk. Just give them this." I touch the register screen and produce the QR code. "Scan it onto your phone and show it to your Customer Courtesy Service Desk Concierge, who will provide the key to the lock after the purchase is finalized." I watch the register screen while the inventory adjusts. I place the gun, the ammunition, and the ticket in a bright AllMART bag, size small, extra tough. "Is there anything else I can help you with today? There are some fantastic sales in the meat department. The hot-stone massages at the salon are to die for. . . ."

"To die for," says the customer. She shoves the shopping bag in her purse and starts walking away toward the front of the store.

"Don't forget to stop by the service desk to complete your shopping experience," I say. "They will remove the trigger lock and deactivate the senso-tag so you can exit without alarm." I don't want this to slip her mind. I don't want her to become an accidental shoplifter, which would reduce my completed sales for the day. Watching her walk away, I see now that I really should have emphasized the hot-stone massage. It would have been an excellent choice for her. Better than the meat sale. She needs to relax. I need to be more sensitive to the needs of the individual customer. I need to read them better.

I wish I'd been able to direct her exit through another department, but I shouldn't be too hard on myself. I up-sold her on the pink special model, and the box of ammunition was large, not small. I reach under the counter and get out my bottle of glass cleaner and the polishing cloth. Every smudge of fingerprint is gone. It is as if the lovely customer were never here. Then I call up the inventory readout on the sale, just to double-check everything, although the computer never makes mistakes. That's when I notice that the pink gun was the last one in stock. I type in the warehouse order.

"Item is permanently out of stock."

I look at the guns arranged on the black velvet. It is impossible not to notice that something is missing. I distribute all of the remaining guns so the case looks full instead of empty. I don't want customers to think that they are deprived of anything. I want them to feel confident that their visit to the Great Outdoors has provided them with the full shopping experience. I want them to feel satisfied.

5er meets me at the door with a box of cereal in his hand. I hold up an AllMART bag full of shelf-safe boxes of milk. He shakes the cereal box. I walk to the sink where our bowls and spoons are sitting, rinsed and ready. Cereal is the extent of my cooking. 5er doesn't complain about the menu.

I carry both bowls back to the table where 5er likes to perch. He climbs up, squats, and puts his hands out. Dinner is served. I lean one butt cheek on the edge of the table and start eating. The room-temperature milk is sad. I look at the pink bunnies running around the edge of my bowl. Poor bunnies, they never get anywhere. They just go around and around like socks in a dryer or an AllMART trainee trying to get out of debt.

≡ *CHANNEL 42* ≡

!UPDATE! !UPDATE! !UPDATE!

Voice-over: **This evening, part one of a very special two-part special on surveillance and security.**

Scene: **Drone hovers over burning house. Close-up on street security camera. It swivels. We can see the lens adjust the focus.**

Voice-over: **With Chad Manley and Sallie Lee.**

Chad Manley: **Tonight we are going to show you the wonders of security. Like this.**

(Camera tight on Manley holding a small object between thumb and finger.)

This **is the most powerful weapon against crime. Seriously, more powerful than a bullet. That's right; amazing, isn't it? This is a video transmitter no bigger than a mint. Would you care for a mint, Sallie? Oops. Dropped it.**

(Camera follows falling object.)

What color are your panties, Sallie? Well, let's see.

(Feed changes to micro-camera.)

They're black, folks—as you can see for yourselves. It's remarkable, high-definition imagery broadcast in real time.

Sallie Lee: **This is not news, Chad.**

Chad Manley: **It is to me. Sanjay and I thought you were more of a commando chick.**

Sallie Lee: **Sanjay, Bag Baby surveillance video, now.**

209

It is me, and there I am, dropping that bag and running away. There is a bright spot that highlights me in the crowd, but it is still impossible to see my face. It doesn't matter how many times they show it; I am nobody.

> **Sallie Lee:** We've all seen this, but it isn't all there is to see. Channel 42 has been given the right to show you newly discovered surveillance video. We will share it with you tomorrow, in part two of this very special special.

(Screen shot of nighttime traffic viewed from drone.)

> **Chad Manley:** Ah, shit, Sallie, you're a journalist. You know that up-skirt video feed is protected as free speech. Get over it.

There must have been other cameras. There are cameras everywhere. There might have been a drone above me. There might have been someone doing self-surveillance with a phone who caught me and the bag in the crowd. My fingerprint may not be in any system, but my face? If there is a glimpse of my face in any footage, facial recognition software can match me to my crime.

If I tell Timmer, he will try to help. That's why I can't tell him. There is no doubt what is coming, and it is coming for me. I'm the one. I left the baby in the bag on the sidewalk.

Nothing can save me. If Timmer tries to hold on to me, it will be like one satellite touching another; we will all shatter and fall. I have only one choice. I have to be arrested for my crime, and the best thing to do is make that very easy. I just have to be where I'm supposed to be — behind the gun counter in AllMART's Great Outdoors.

That night I read from the book about the Martians.

"Tumbleweed. Fragile. Names," says the book.

I hope 5er remembers when I'm gone.

He puts his hands on my cheeks.

He doesn't say a word, but then, he never does.

22

It is quiet in the store this morning.

I can hear the sparrows flutter overhead. They are building a nest on top of the surveillance camera. I worry. It doesn't look like a safe place to raise babies to me, but there is nothing I can do about it.

I take out the spray cleaner and start polishing the glass over the guns. The sparrows tend to leave a mess down here below. I will need to get a ladder and clean the top of the polar bear's case too. These are the consequences of changing Kral's bird-murdering policy. These are the consequences of choosing life. Worry and messes.

There is a rumbling noise. An odd one—not the sound of a warehouse ladder, not the sound of a forklift groaning to life.

It is the sound of running feet.

Men in black body armor are rushing down the aisle.

They are coming for me.

There is nothing I can do about it.

I knew this moment was coming.

They move in formation, but there isn't enough room for that. The endcap display of canoe paddles crashes down. The stampede is over as quickly as it began.

I move out from behind the counter and begin picking up the paddles.

The men in black armor will discover their error and come back for me soon. There is no point in running. I can't outrun them. There is no point in taking the keys, removing a nice little gun, and putting up a fight. I can't outgun them. So I do what I can do; I let ZERO tidy up the aisle. It could have been worse. Paddles don't shatter. It's an easy cleanup.

Overhead, a camera drone wobbles and dips in the air. The sparrows flutter.

I'm sliding the last paddle back into place when I see them returning. I take a deep breath and wait, standing right in the middle of the aisle. The first of them pushes me along in front of him until I fall out of the way. The black force sweeps by, and in the middle there is someone being dragged along, stumbling, blind. They have put an AllMART bag over her head, but I know her. It is Juliette.

The clumsy black suits collide and jostle for space. Things are pushed over; the destruction is contagious, a chain reaction. The polar bear teeters and topples. The glass case shatters and the broken glass shines like a thousand diamond rings. I pull myself back up onto my feet. I turn and lift the intercom handset. "Cleanup on Aisle 125, the Great Outdoors," I say. My voice is calm and patient as a recording. I don't want to alarm or confuse the customers. Then the handset slips out of my hand, and I slide against the wall until I'm curled up on the Ergo-Rest mat that absorbs the painful pressure of being on my feet all day.

It takes all day to put the Great Outdoors in order. The broken glass is swept away, but it seems to leave a ghost behind. I move my head slightly so it catches the light. A sparkle party where I last saw Juliette, the trace of silver glitter from her shoes.

Finally, my shift is ended. I can clock out and go home.

So that's what I do.

I slide my badge through the scanner, walk out the employee exit, and then go around to the front of the store. I walk with purpose across the parking lot. I climb the stairs to the pedestrian bridge. I pass over all that traffic. And I'm invisible. I'm even invisible to a drone that flies up and over the mesh of the bridge. I am invisible because no one is interested in my story.

I'm not the Bag Baby.

I'm not the Girl Who Was/n't Eaten by a Tuna.

I'm just AllMART employee ZERO.

I walk back across the bridge, then I circle around the parking lot. I circle until I arrive home, at the Warren.

"Can we save her?"

No one answers because we know the answer. The answer is no.

We are all together, standing shoulder to shoulder watching Channel 42.

Over and over again, the camera shows us Juliette, dragged blind and stumbling out of our world.

We share this heartbreak. In this way we are all united.

But the camera doesn't show everything. It doesn't see that Juliette's shoes are falling apart, and that, after she is gone, there is a little track of glitter that marks her passing. The drone surveils, but it doesn't hear her calling softly for Raoul. The camera doesn't know what I know: that Juliette did the right thing. She saw someone who needed help, and she gave it, best as she could.

The camera never does see those things.

And there's still no verdict in the tuna-girl custody case, and the dark neighborhoods are still on fire, and ammunition is in short supply, and tonight we should all look up to see the shiny sparkle of the satellite rain.

23

≡ CHANNEL 42 ≡

!UPDATE! !UPDATE! !UPDATE!

Voice-over: This evening, the exciting conclusion of Channel 42's very special two-part special on surveillance and security.

Scene: Drone hovers over burning house. Close-up on street security camera. It swivels and we can see the lens adjust the focus.

Voice-over: With Chad Manley and Sallie Lee.

They run new video of the arrest. We see more this time. Through the drone we see Juliette being grabbed at her station at Fancy ManiPedis, the bag pulled over her head, the moment when they tased her and she collapsed, a small bright figure swallowed by a churning clot of black helmets.

Sallie Lee: And now, an exclusive, the surveillance evidence that cracked this case wide open.

That night, Juliette never thought about surveillance. Her eyes were on the baby, and that baby was her blind spot. We see her close up, cradling it in her arms, and though we can't hear what she is saying, there is so much tenderness in her face when she rubs her cheek against that drowsy lump of baby that it makes my insides ache. We see her gather things the baby might need, we see her winding through the aisles of AllMART, we see her exit, and we see her walk away with unswerving purpose.

We see her walk straight toward the Warren.

She broke Raoul's rule. She walked directly home. And what this means we don't yet know, but it cannot be good.

Sallie Lee: There's the video evidence. The surveillance camera tells the whole story.

Chad Manley: Looks like case closed to me.

Sallie Lee: I think this time — for the first time — you're right, Chad.

Chad Manley: (Grinning.) Hey, Sallie, would you like to see the story I reported with my personal drone camera last night? Sure you would. . . . Roll that beautiful drone footage, Sanjay.

Scene: Drone ascends past the light and dark windows of a tall apartment building. Hovers outside the slender window to a bathroom. Inside is Sallie Lee, naked with her hands braced against the toilet tank, vomiting.

Chad Manley: Again, isn't that resolution amazing?

Scene: In-studio close-up on Sallie Lee. She stands. The camera is unprepared for the change. It is an unscripted moment. Without the smooth zoom-out for the longer shot, Sallie Lee's face isn't visible. Her hand points a pink gun straight at the camera.

ZERO knows that model of gun. It is a *kawaii* accessory. It can fit in a small purse. Sadly, it is out of stock and future orders cannot be filled. Sad. It's adorable. And demand will

218

be high now that the television audience sees how adorable it looks in Sallie Lee's hand.

The gunshots sound louder than most heard on the Channel 42 News. I guess that's because these aren't recorded and volume controlled. The sound is being picked up live through the mic clipped to Sallie Lee's business-fashion corset.

Scene: **News studio. The camera wobbles out of control. It's a dizzy look at the studio until it settles, lens down, unfocused.**

What is that? What? It takes a while to see, but I'm pretty sure that is Sanjay on the floor, although I've never seen him before. Sanjay was a behind-the-camera guy, until now. Sanjay is dying on live television. But then the segment loops and repeats. Sanjay dies again. He was the behind-the-camera guy. He was probably in charge of switching from feed to feed. Now that he is dead on the studio floor, who knows which button to press to change it to a different feed? Sanjay may be getting shot for hours.

"Guys," says Luck. "Guys, we need to go."

And Luck is absolutely right.

"We're heading east," says Pineapple, pointing to the place where the sun will surely rise.

"We'll go some other way," says Timmer.

"See you," says Pineapple, like it is possible our orbits might touch again.

"Bring it in," says Timmer. "Bring it in." And he opens his arms wide. We all huddle and hold one another close.

"What we got," says Timmer, "is yours."

Pineapple and Luck each take a box of cereal.

"Gas money," says Timmer, and he holds a card out to Pineapple.

"Man, can't do it."

"No!" says Timmer. "You damn well will!"

Pineapple takes the card.

"But there's a condition," says Timmer. "The deal is you be looking. You be looking for the ones you need to help." That's when Timmer buckles. He puts his hand over his eyes and his shoulders shake.

"That's the deal," says Luck.

Then Pineapple and Luck get into their car. The back-seat is level, full of clothes and cereal boxes and useful stuff. They're gone.

Timmer puts his arm around my shoulder. "Hey! You! Last Girl. Where you want to go? There is no bus to Terra Incognita. I can give you a ride."

"I don't want to go to Terra Incognita; I want to go to Mars. . . ."

"I don't have that much gas," says Timmer.

"Well then, just take me home."

Before the sun sets and the frilly underpants of the sky

touch the naked rock of the mountains, I see a plume of black smoke rising reflected in the rearview mirror. It might be a scrap yard. It might be a laundromat.

"Earth seemed to explode, catch fire, and burn," says the book.

We drive north. I hold my badge out the window and it flippy-floppy-flips in the speeding air until I let it go and then it's gone. That's the end of ZERO.

My pillowcase is at my feet. Inside are my underpants, my pink bunny bowl, and the book about Mars. We have boxes of cereal, jugs of water, and an orange plastic can that's almost full of gas. Kral wouldn't be impressed, but we have what we need to survive right now.

We drive, and the desert is full of nothing, miles and miles of empty AllMART bags caught on the twiggy weeds. When we come to the exit for the Villages at Moonrise River Meadows, the moon does rise, and light on the road shines like a river. The little LED candle flickers on the windowsill. Timmer parks and says, "Home. For tonight."

We walk in the front door, and the voice of the house says, "Welcome home. Welc." It falls silent. Dust on the solar panels has starved the house of power. It has nothing to say. In the dim light, I see the fake cake right where we left it.

"We will drink some water, 5er. And I'll read to you until we lose the light."

"The whole damn planet belongs to us, kids. The whole darn planet," says the book.

I don't know if 5er understands the words. I don't know if I understand the words. But we both understand that this is a way to care for each other.

In the morning, the sky is a melted mirror. I step out onto the balcony, where Timmer is standing. He turns to me and smiles, his hands open palm in front of him, like the world is a gift, like he created all of this for me. If there is any living thing in the world except the two of us, it doesn't matter. Dust is sifting into the waiting craters of basements and bone-dry swimming pools. This moment will last forever. Our shadows stretch out, wavering and thin.

The dust on the roof can't bear the weight of sunlight, and it breaks free, slides off the blue solar panels like wrinkled silk, avalanches down the red clay tiles. The falling dust makes no sound. The air is still as glass, and the smallest motes shimmer in the early light. Timmer reaches out to touch my face.

My phone rings.

After all this time, all this waiting, someone is calling out to me. . . .

. . . *ZeeZeeBee! You need to come to the city right now! You could find a great job—easy-peasy—or you can go back to school! Either way. But I can't live without my baby Zoëkins. Please come. I miss you so much. I miss you thirty-seven pink socks and a bowl of cereal. So, so much!*

. . . *Hello, my name is Ed Gorton. I think . . . Damn, this isn't easy. I think maybe . . . I'm your dad.*

. . . Zoë, this is Dawna Day, your personal human-resources manager. Please, make this easy. Let me help you. You'll be helping me too. That's what families do. They help and care for each other. Just tell me where you are. . . . I don't think you understand, Zoë; you are a human resource of AllMART. And until you return to AllMART, you are in illegal possession of property that belongs to AllMART. If you don't return to AllMART custody in twenty-four hours, I have to press charges for felony theft. Please don't make me do that.

I pick up the phone, still singing unanswered, and throw it out into the empty world. There is a little explosion of dust when it lands.

There is no ZeeZeeBee, no ZERO—there isn't even a Zoë. There is only me, Z. I am the last girl, and I don't want closure. I want to see how Timmer and 5er go on. That's what interests me. I want to be there when 5er wakes and looks open-eyed at the dark. I want to be there when a pearl of water rests at the bottom of Timmer's backbone. I want to be there when satellites kiss and fall like burning butterflies. The sparkle of satellite rain means the end of something, but not everything. It is not the end of me. It is not the end of Z, the last living girl in Terra Incognita.

ACKNOWLEDGMENTS

Liz Bicknell and Candlewick Press gave me the opportunity to write this book. Without her vision and the support Candlewick provided, there wouldn't be a *MARTians*. Special thanks to copy editor Betsy Uhrig and designer Sherry Fatla, who brought all the media to life through typography—I owe those women roses for their hard work. Carter Hasegawa, who sought permission for the Bradbury quotes, has my eternal gratitude. Matt Roeser designed the cover—judging by that, *MARTians* is a fine book indeed.

I also acknowledge a debt to my Clarion West class and instructor Connie Willis. I will never forget the time I shared with you during the summer of the apricot moon.

Sarah Davies of Greenhouse Agency was, as always, the best fairy godmother in publishing.

Finally, my family takes care of me and forgives me more often than they should. Everything I do depends on that.